ARIOL

D0038939

CALGARY PUBLIC LIBRARY

MAY - - 2015

PAPERCUTZ ™

ARiOL Graphic Novels available from PAPERCUTZ™

ARIOL graphic novels are also available digitally wherever e-books are sold.

Emmanuel Guibert
Marc Boutavant
ARiOL
Just a Donkey Like You and Me
PAPERCUTZ

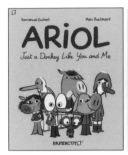

Graphic Novel #1
"Just a Donkey Like You and Me"

ARiOL

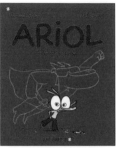

Graphic Novel #2
"Thunder Horse"

Emmanuel Guibert
Marc Boutavant
ARiOL
Happy as a Pig...
PAPERCUTZ

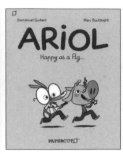

Graphic Novel #3
"Happy as a Pig..."

ARiOL

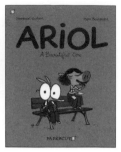

Graphic Novel #4
"A Beautiful Cow"

ARiOL
Bizzbilla Hits the Bullseye
PAPERCUTZ

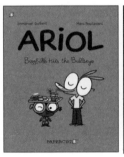

Graphic Novel #5
"Bizzbilla Hits the Bullseye"

ARiOL

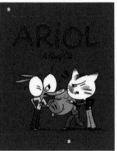

Graphic Novel #6
"A Nasty Cat"

Emmanuel Guibert
Marc Boutavant
ARiOL
Boxed Set of Graphic Novels #1-3
PAPERCUTZ

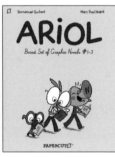

Boxed Set of Graphic Novels #1-3

Emmanuel Guibert
Marc Boutavant
ARiOL
Where's PETULA?
PAPERCUTZ

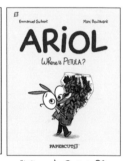

"Where's Petula?" Graphic Novel

Coming Soon

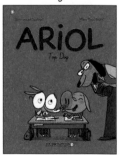

ARiOL
Top Dog

Ariol #7
"Top Dog"

ARIOL graphic novels are available for $12.99 only in paperback, except for "Where's Petula?" which is $9.99. The ARIOL Boxed Set is $38.99. Available from booksellers everywhere. You can also order online from papercutz.com. Or call 1-800-886-1223, Monday through Friday, 9-5 EST. MC, Visa and AmEx accepted. To order by mail, please add $4.00 for postage and handling for first book ordered, $1.00 for each additional book and make check payable to NBM Publishing. Send to:
Papercutz, 160 Broadway, Suite 700, East Wing, New York, NY 10038.

papercutz.com

Emmanuel Guibert   Marc Boutavant

ARIOL

Where's Petula?

PAPERCUTZ™
New York

To madame Trébon
– Emmanuel Guibert

ARIOL
Where's Petula?

Emmanuel Guibert – Writer
Marc Boutavant – Artist
Rémi Chaurand – Colorist
Joe Johnson – Translation
Bryan Senka – Letterer
Jeff Whitman – Production Coordinator
Beth Scorzato – Editor
Noah Sharma – Editorial Intern

Jim Salicrup
Editor-in-Chief

Ariol: Où est PÉTULA?
© Bayard Editions Jeunesse, 2013

ISBN: 978-1-62991-186-1

Printed in China
April 2015 by O.G. Printing Productions, LTD.
Units 2 & 3, 5/F, Lemmi Centre
50 Hoi Yuen Road
Kwon Tong, Kowloon

Papercutz books may be purchased for business or promotional use. For information on bulk purchases please contact
Macmillan Corporate and Premium Sales Department at (800) 221-7945 x5442.

Distributed by Macmillan
First Papercutz Printing

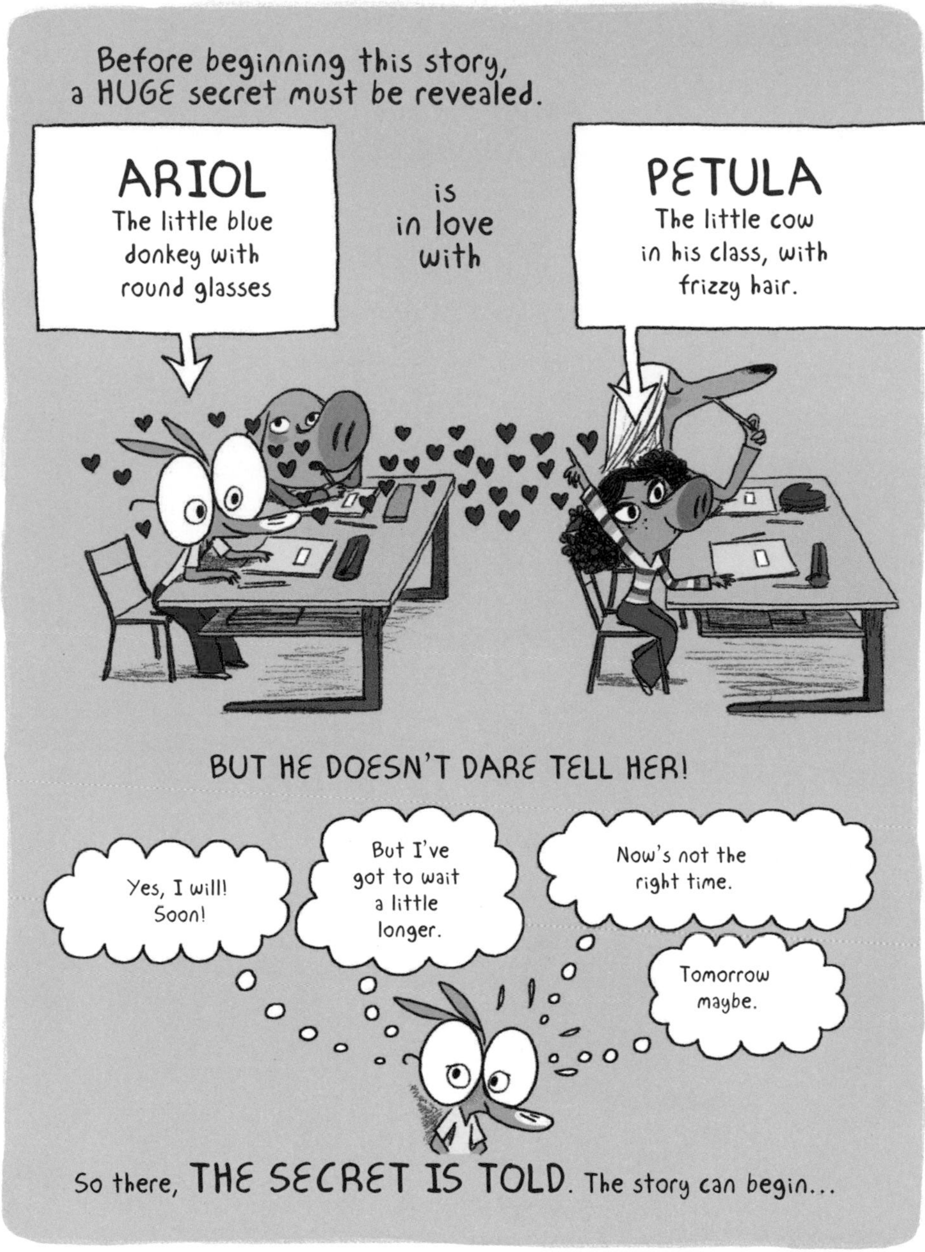
Before beginning this story, a HUGE secret must be revealed.
ARIOL The little blue donkey with round glasses
is in love with
PETULA The little cow in his class, with frizzy hair.
BUT HE DOESN'T DARE TELL HER!
Yes, I will! Soon!
But I've got to wait a little longer.
Now's not the right time.
Tomorrow maybe.
So there, THE SECRET IS TOLD. The story can begin...

CHAPTER 1

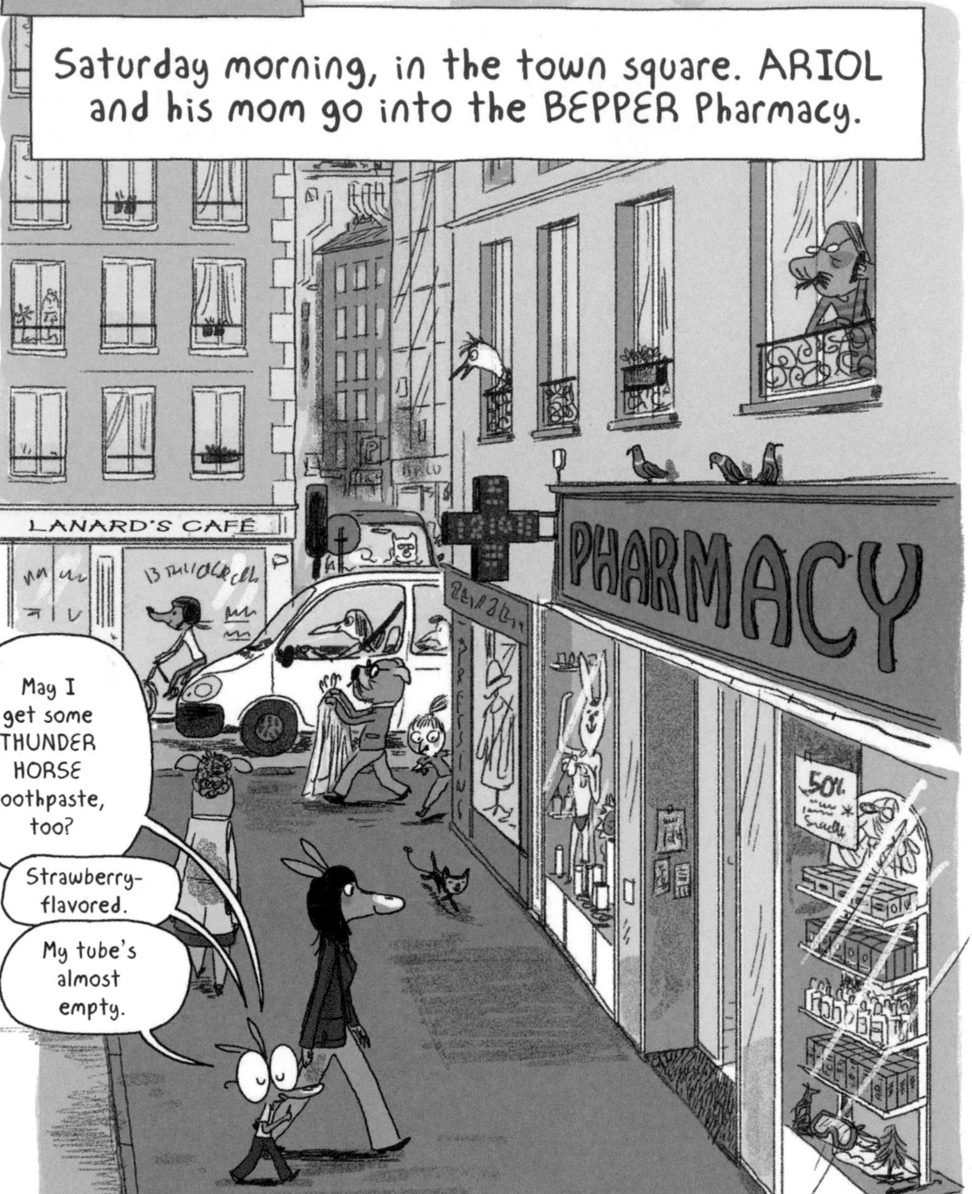
Saturday morning, in the town square. ARIOL and his mom go into the BEPPER Pharmacy.
LANARD'S CAFÉ
PHARMACY
50%
May I get some THUNDER HORSE toothpaste, too?
Strawberry-flavored.
My tube's almost empty.

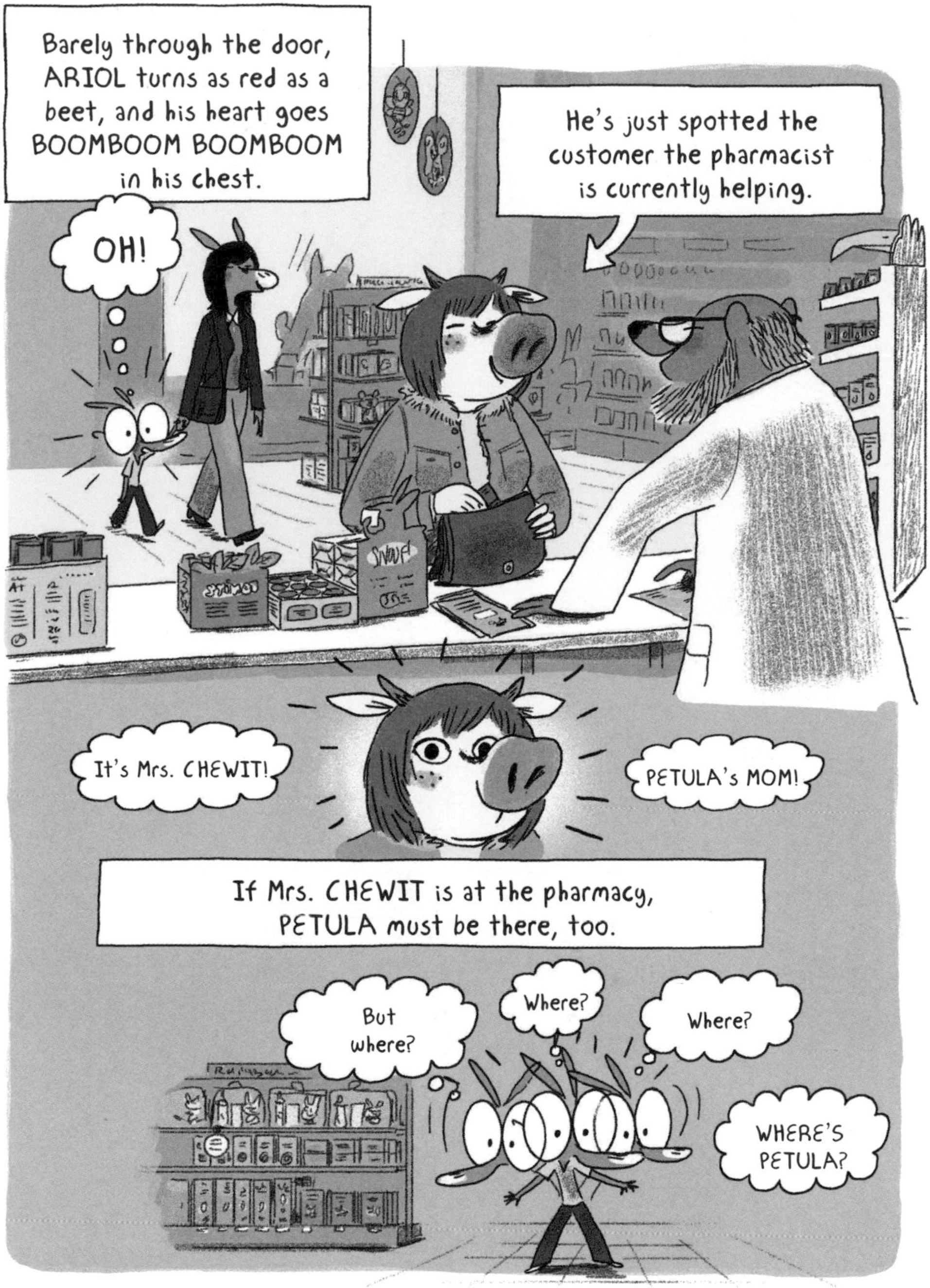
Barely through the door, ARIOL turns as red as a beet, and his heart goes BOOMBOOM BOOMBOOM in his chest.
He's just spotted the customer the pharmacist is currently helping.
OH!
It's Mrs. CHEWIT!
PETULA's MOM!
If Mrs. CHEWIT is at the pharmacy, PETULA must be there, too.
But where?
Where?
Where?
WHERE'S PETULA?

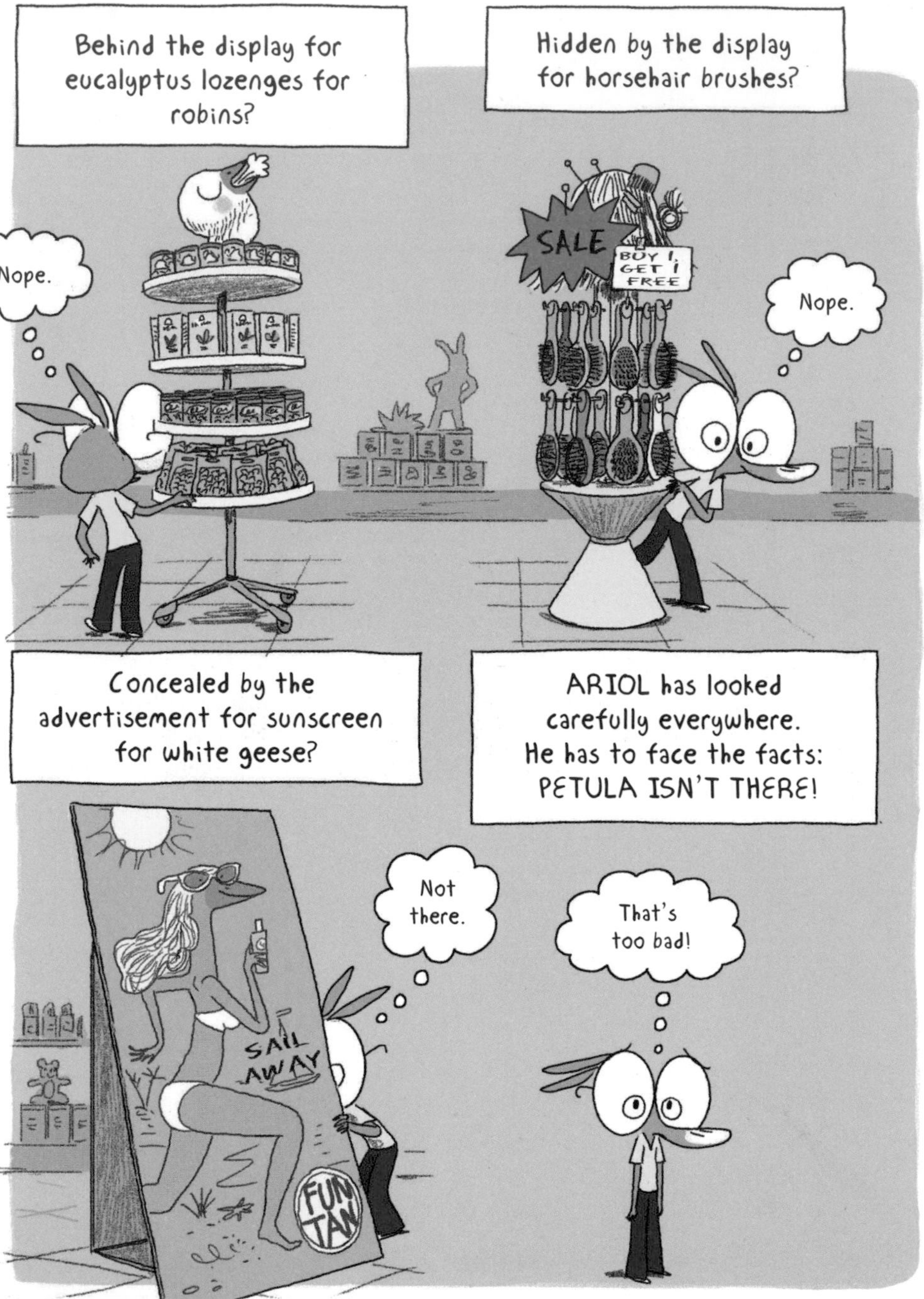
Behind the display for eucalyptus lozenges for robins?
Nope.
Hidden by the display for horsehair brushes?
SALE
BUY 1, GET 1 FREE
Nope.
Concealed by the advertisement for sunscreen for white geese?
SAIL AWAY
FUN TAN
Not there.
ARIOL has looked carefully everywhere.
He has to face the facts:
PETULA ISN'T THERE!
That's too bad!

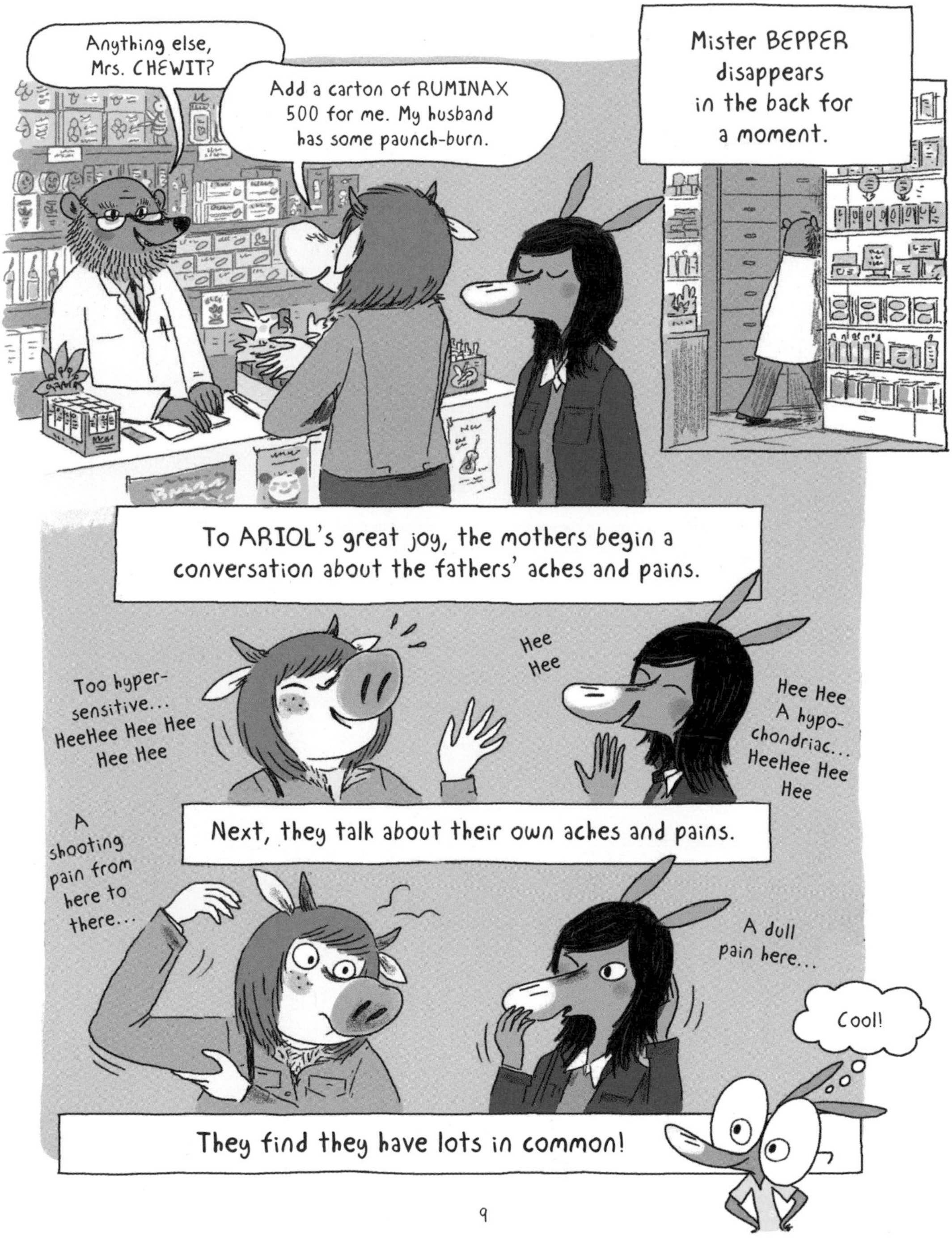

Anything else, Mrs. CHEWIT?
Add a carton of RUMINAX 500 for me. My husband has some paunch-burn.
Mister BEPPER disappears in the back for a moment.
To ARIOL's great joy, the mothers begin a conversation about the fathers' aches and pains.
Too hyper-sensitive... HeeHee Hee Hee Hee Hee
Hee Hee
Hee Hee A hypo-chondriac... HeeHee Hee Hee
Next, they talk about their own aches and pains.
A shooting pain from here to there...
A dull pain here...
Cool!
They find they have lots in common!

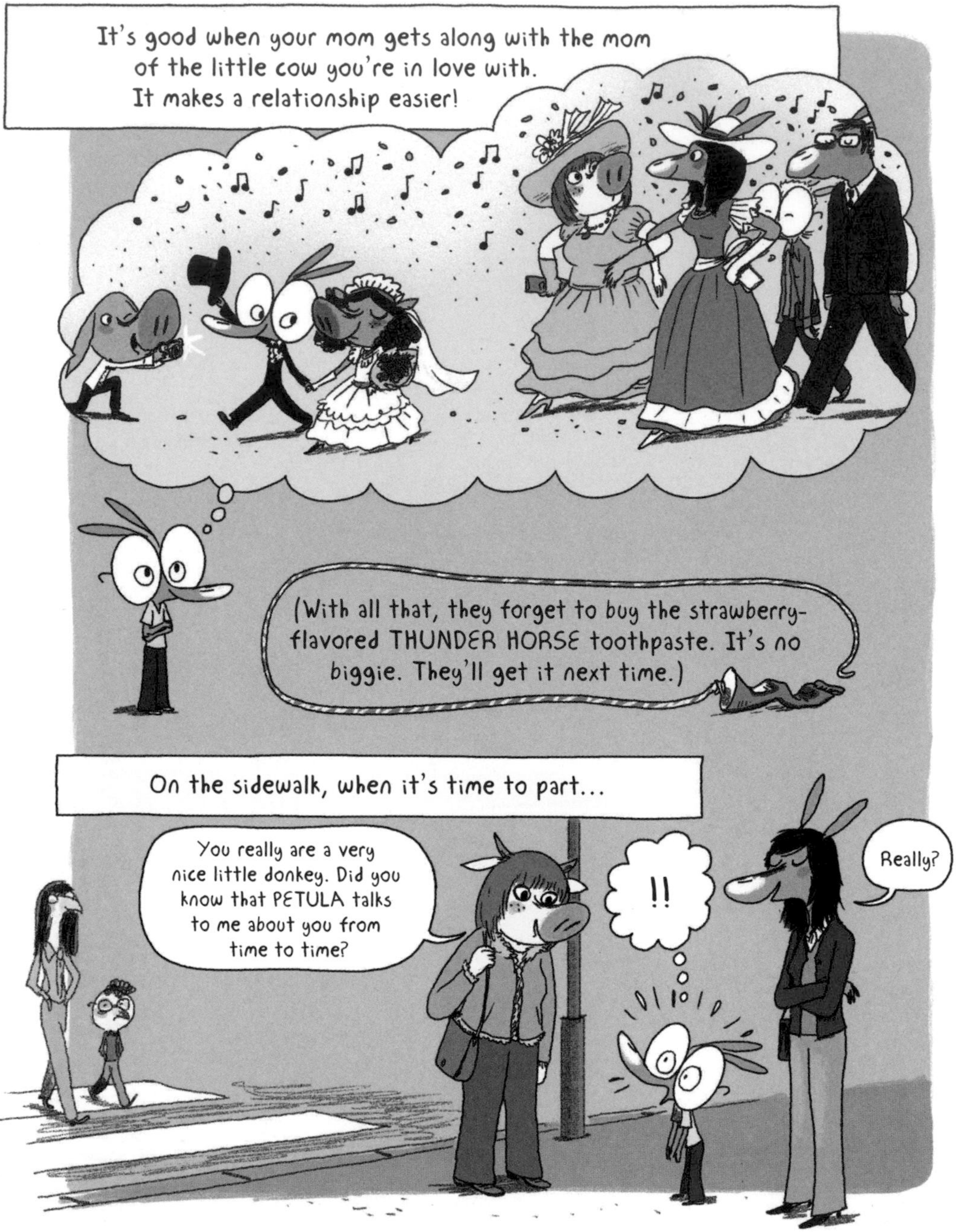
It's good when your mom gets along with the mom of the little cow you're in love with. It makes a relationship easier!
(With all that, they forget to buy the strawberry-flavored THUNDER HORSE toothpaste. It's no biggie. They'll get it next time.)
On the sidewalk, when it's time to part...
You really are a very nice little donkey. Did you know that PETULA talks to me about you from time to time?
!!
Really?

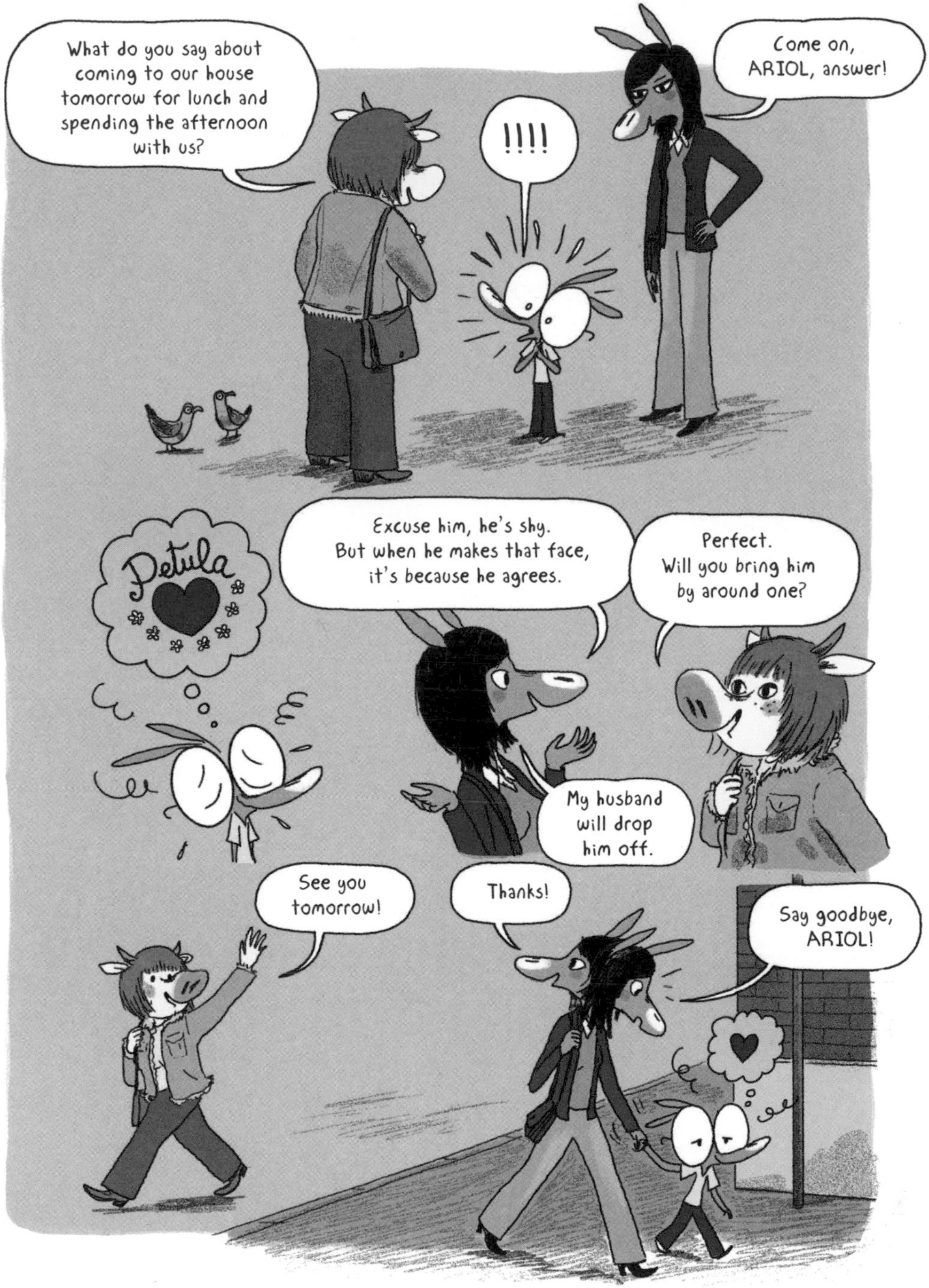
What do you say about coming to our house tomorrow for lunch and spending the afternoon with us?
!!!!
Come on, ARIOL, answer!
Petula
Excuse him, he's shy. But when he makes that face, it's because he agrees.
Perfect. Will you bring him by around one?
My husband will drop him off.
See you tomorrow!
Thanks!
Say goodbye, ARIOL!

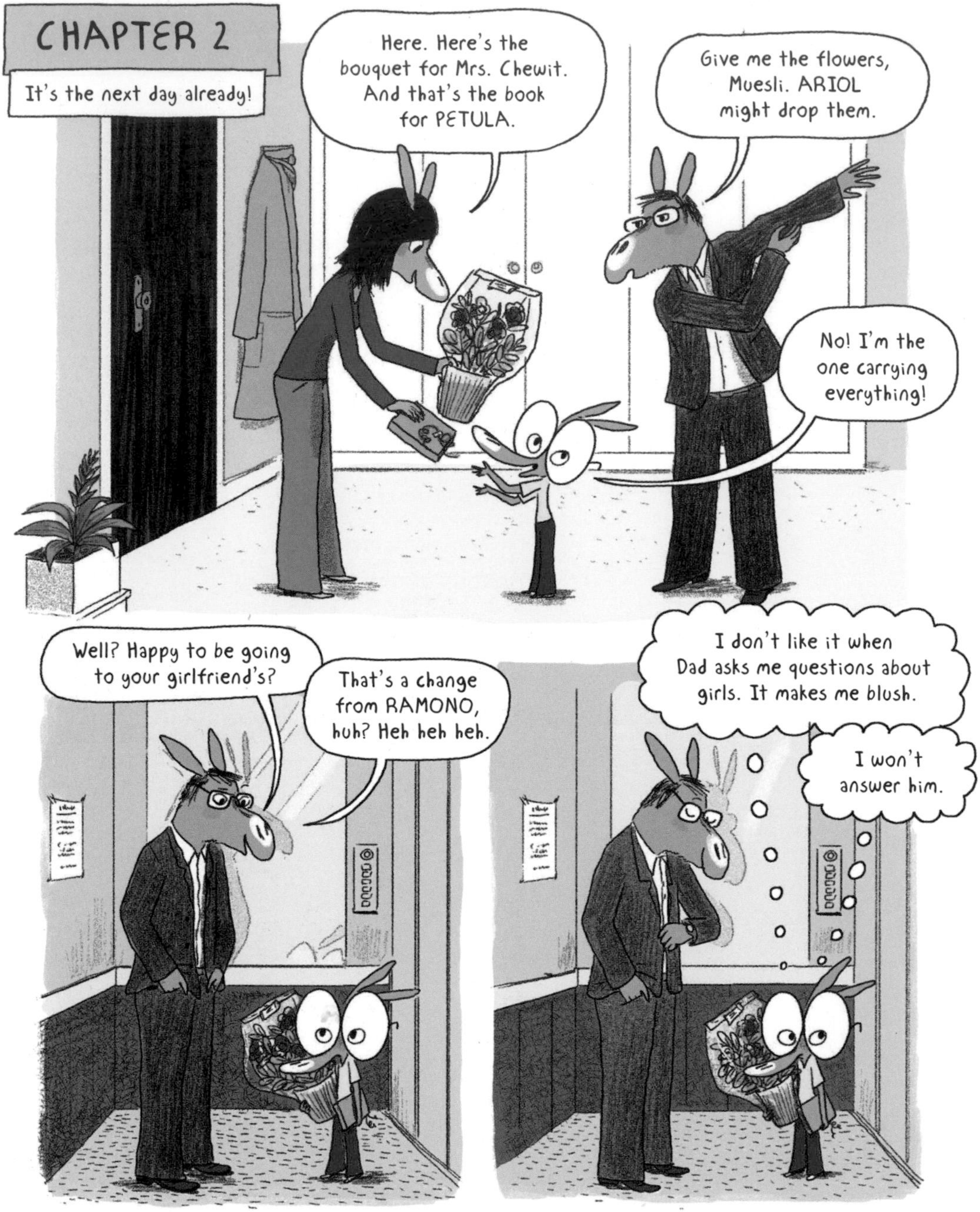
CHAPTER 2
It's the next day already!
Here. Here's the bouquet for Mrs. Chewit. And that's the book for PETULA.
Give me the flowers, Muesli. ARIOL might drop them.
No! I'm the one carrying everything!
Well? Happy to be going to your girlfriend's?
That's a change from RAMONO, huh? Heh heh heh.
I don't like it when Dad asks me questions about girls. It makes me blush.
I won't answer him.

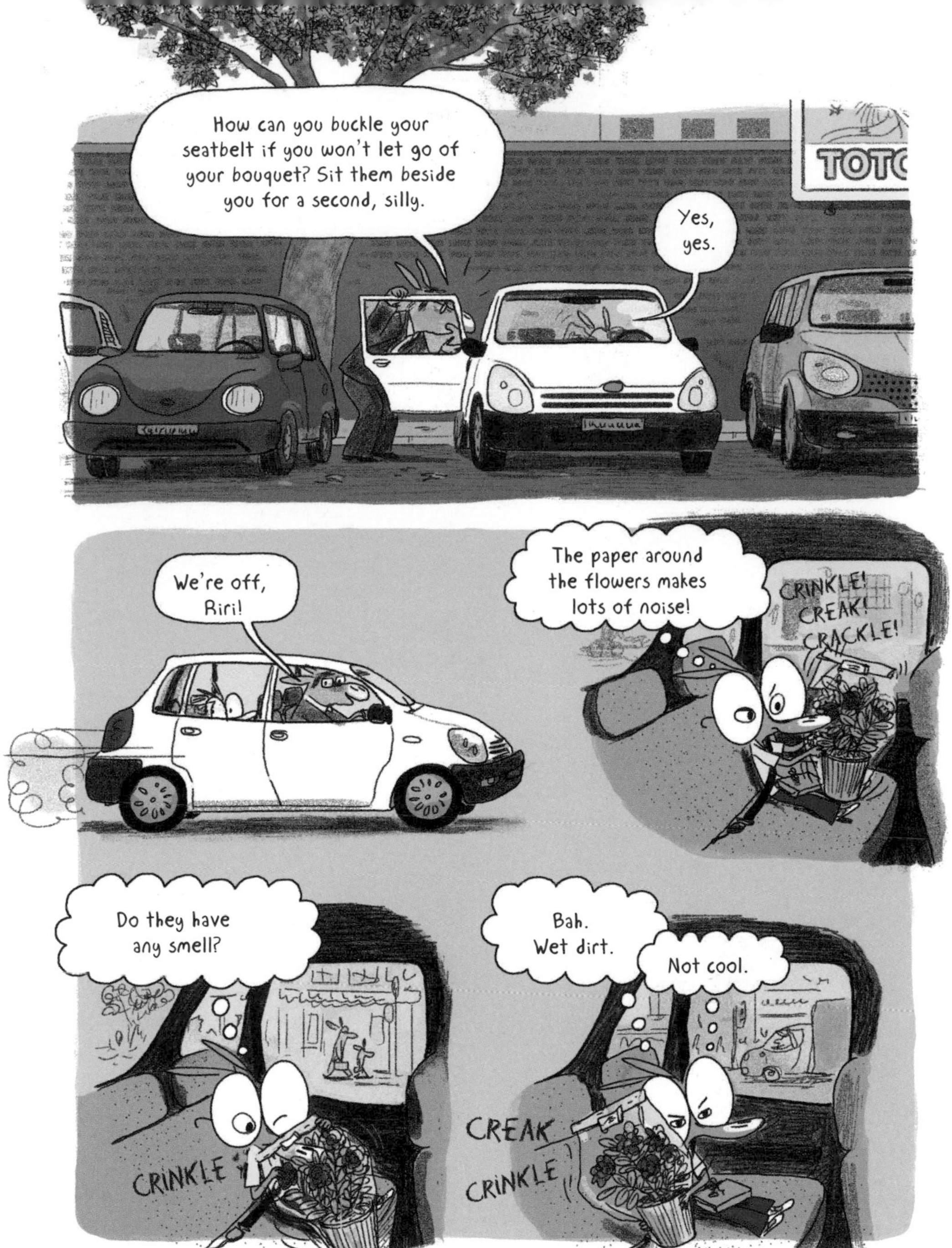

How can you buckle your seatbelt if you won't let go of your bouquet? Sit them beside you for a second, silly.
Yes, yes.
TOTO
We're off, Riri!
The paper around the flowers makes lots of noise!
CRINKLE! CREAK! CRACKLE!
Do they have any smell?
CRINKLE
Bah. Wet dirt.
Not cool.
CREAK
CRINKLE

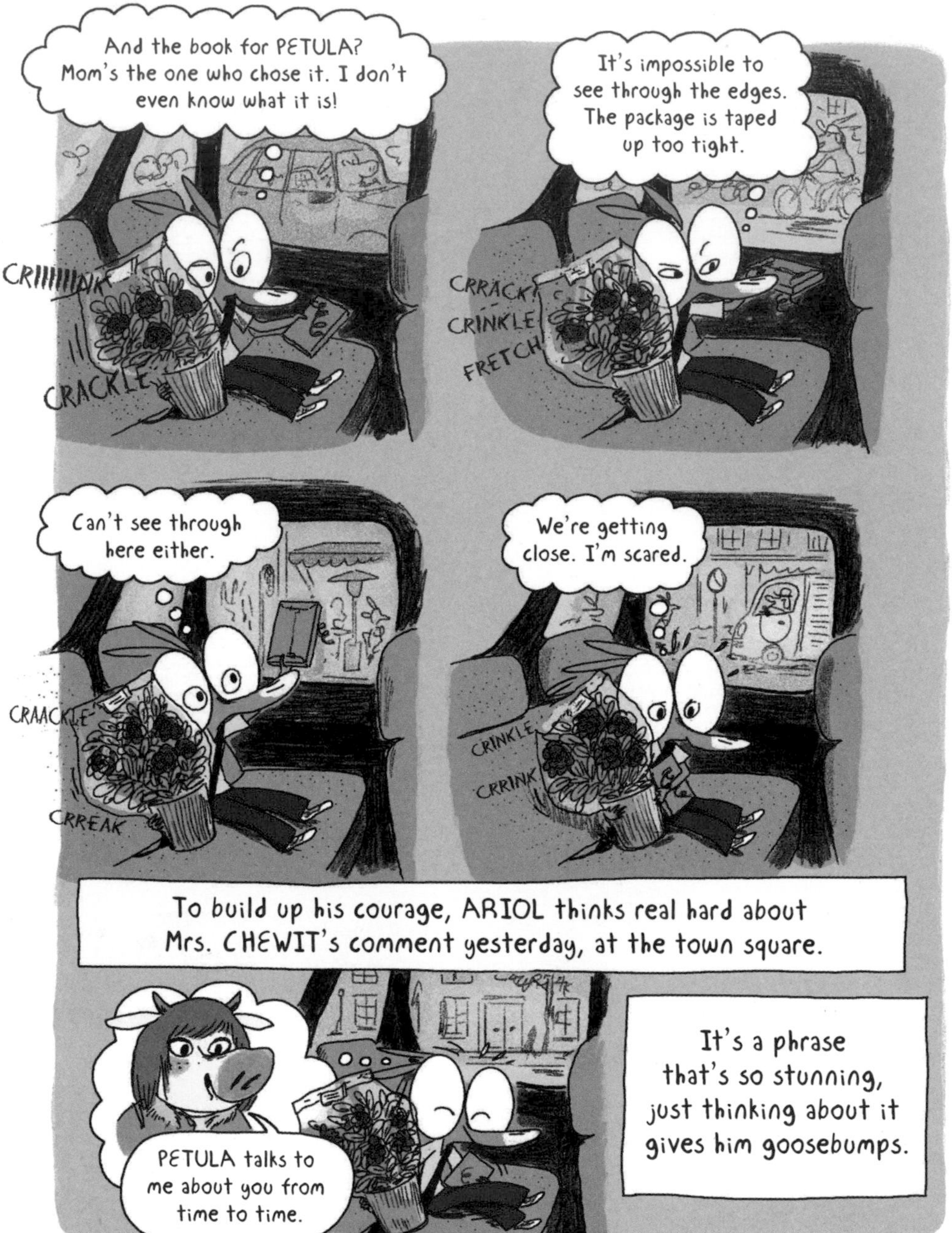
And the book for PETULA? Mom's the one who chose it. I don't even know what it is!
CRIIIIIINK
CRACKLE
It's impossible to see through the edges. The package is taped up too tight.
CRRACK!
CRINKLE
FRETCH
Can't see through here either.
CRAACKLE
CRREAK
We're getting close. I'm scared.
CRINKLE
CRRINK
To build up his courage, ARIOL thinks real hard about Mrs. CHEWIT's comment yesterday, at the town square.
PETULA talks to me about you from time to time.
It's a phrase that's so stunning, just thinking about it gives him goosebumps.

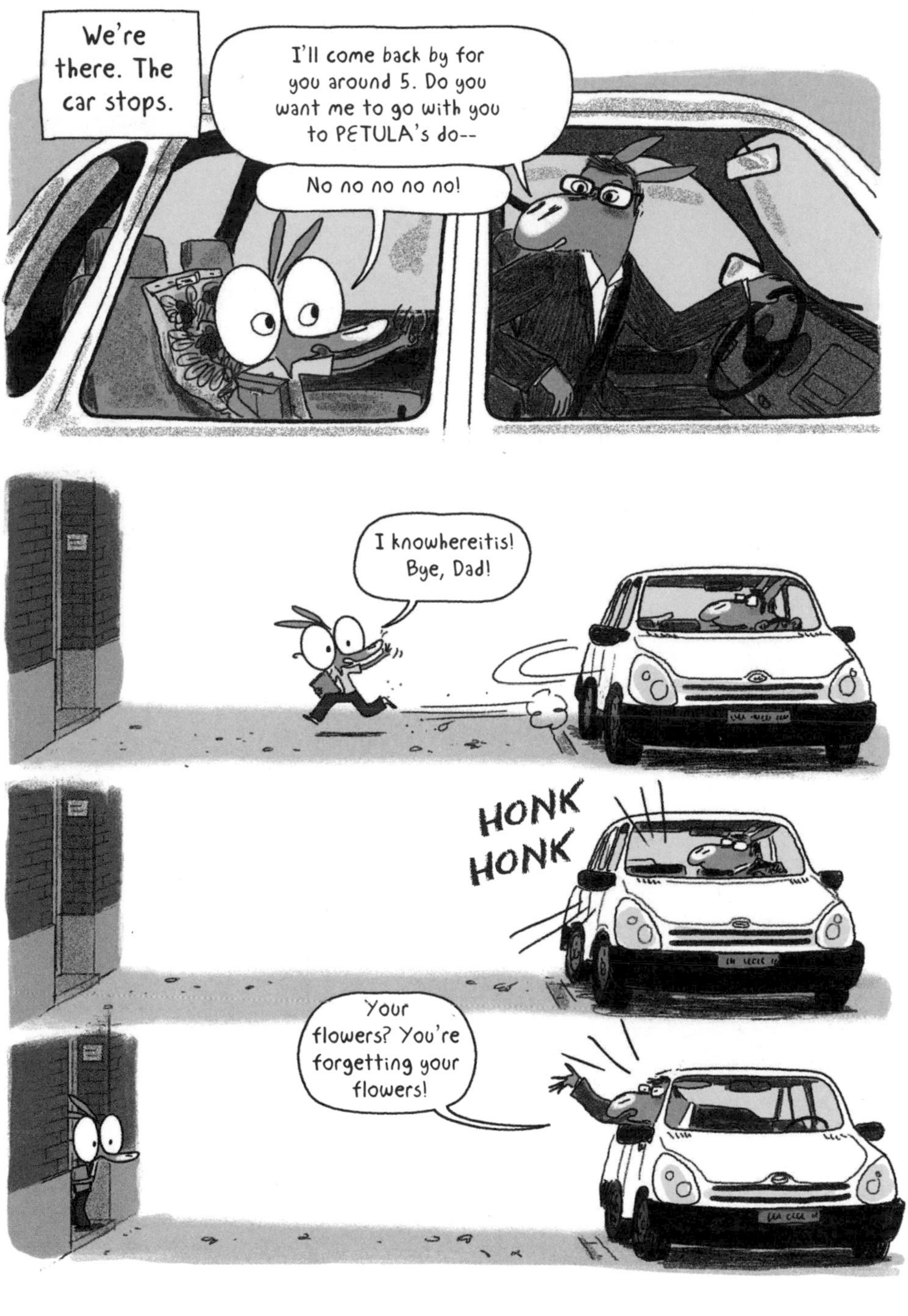
We're there. The car stops.
I'll come back by for you around 5. Do you want me to go with you to PETULA's do--
No no no no no!
I knowhereitis! Bye, Dad!
HONK HONK
Your flowers? You're forgetting your flowers!

CHAPTER 3

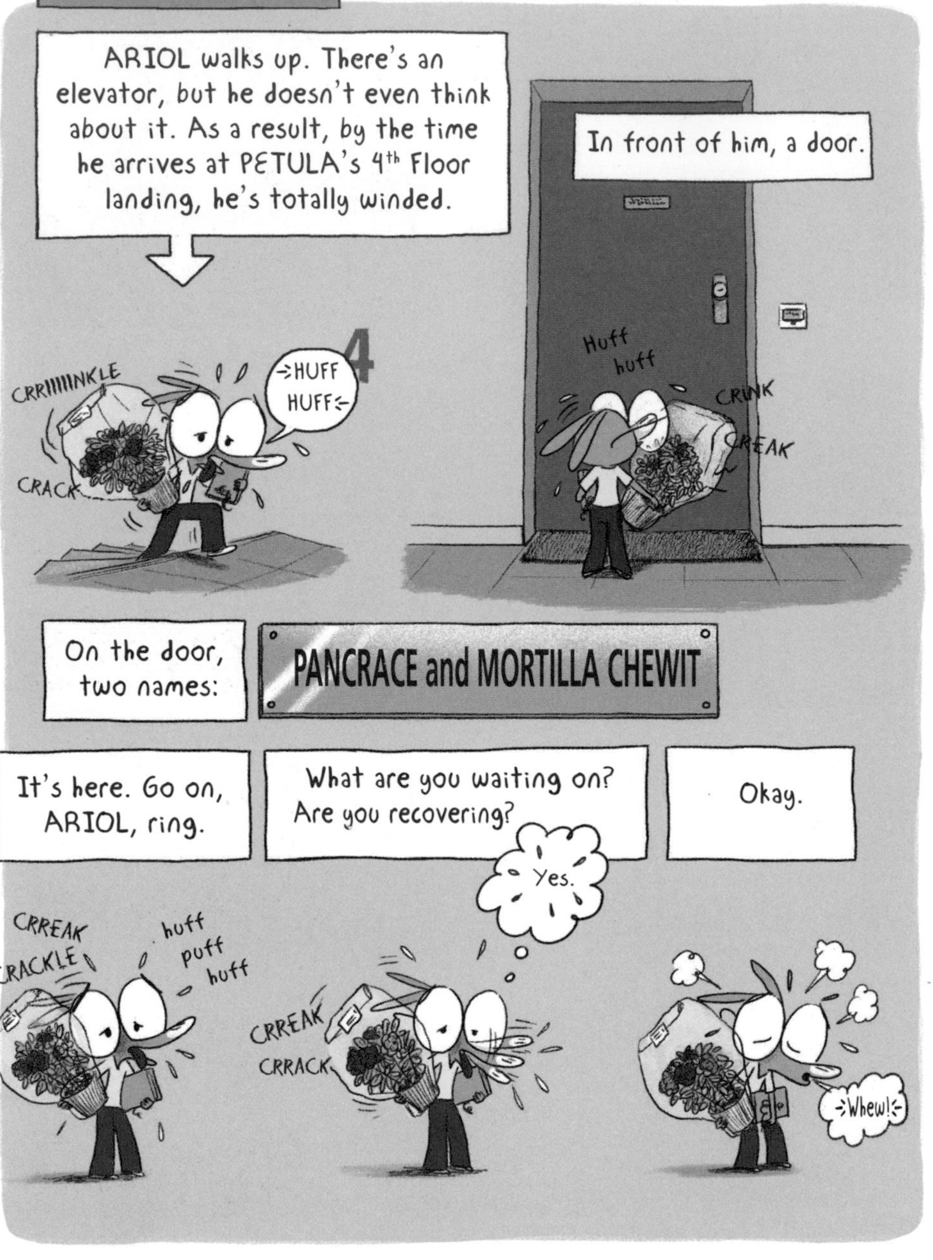
ARIOL walks up. There's an elevator, but he doesn't even think about it. As a result, by the time he arrives at PETULA's 4th Floor landing, he's totally winded.
CRRIIIIINKLE
CRACK
HUFF HUFF
4
In front of him, a door.
Huff huff
CRINK
CREAK
On the door, two names:
PANCRACE and MORTILLA CHEWIT
It's here. Go on, ARIOL, ring.
CRREAK
CRACKLE
huff puff huff
What are you waiting on? Are you recovering?
Yes.
CRREAK
CRRACK
Okay.
Whew!

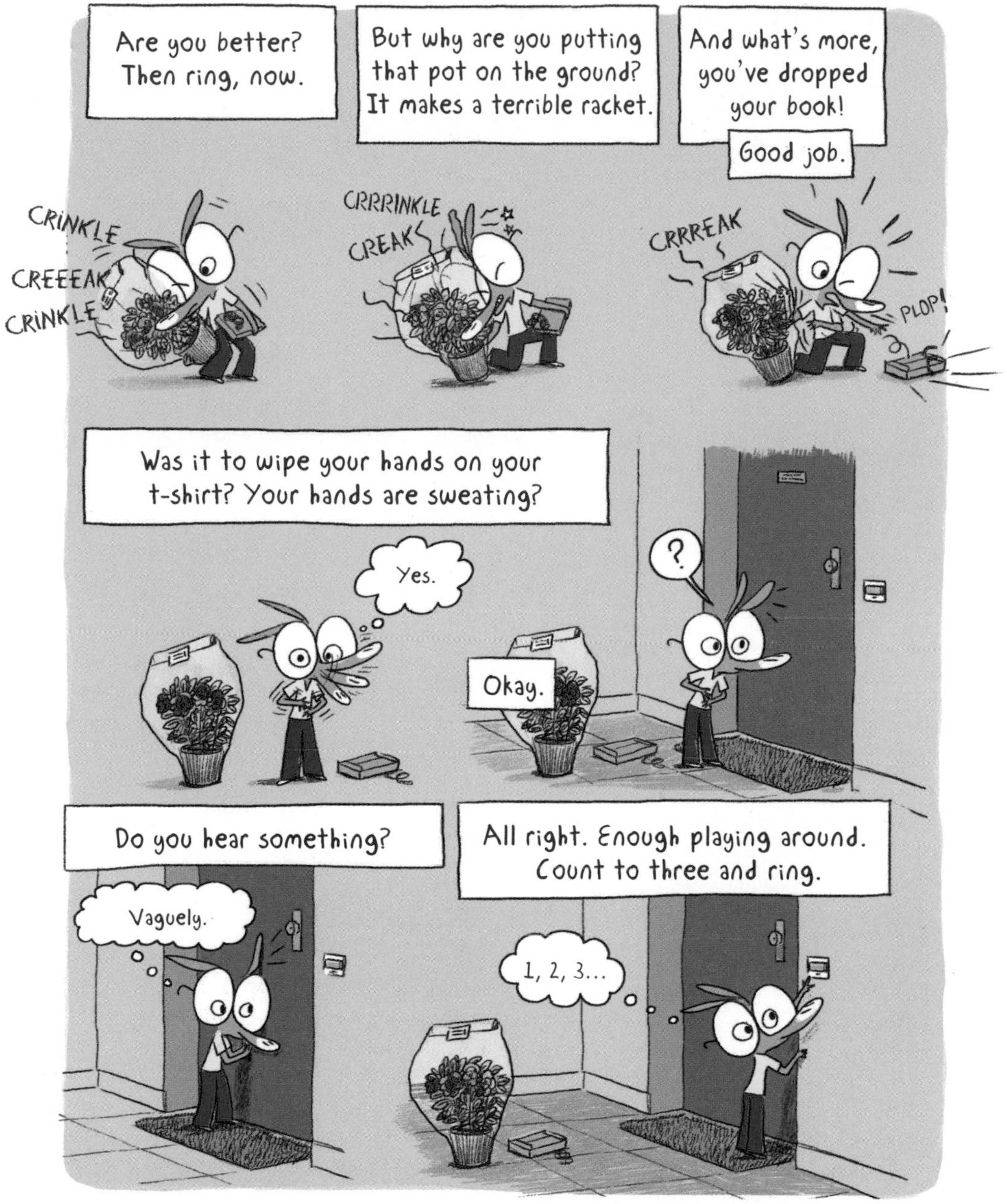
Are you better? Then ring, now.
CRINKLE
CREEEAK
CRINKLE
But why are you putting that pot on the ground? It makes a terrible racket.
CRRRINKLE
CREAK
And what's more, you've dropped your book!
Good job.
CRRREAK
PLOP!
Was it to wipe your hands on your t-shirt? Your hands are sweating?
Yes.
?
Okay.
Do you hear something?
Vaguely.
All right. Enough playing around. Count to three and ring.
1, 2, 3...

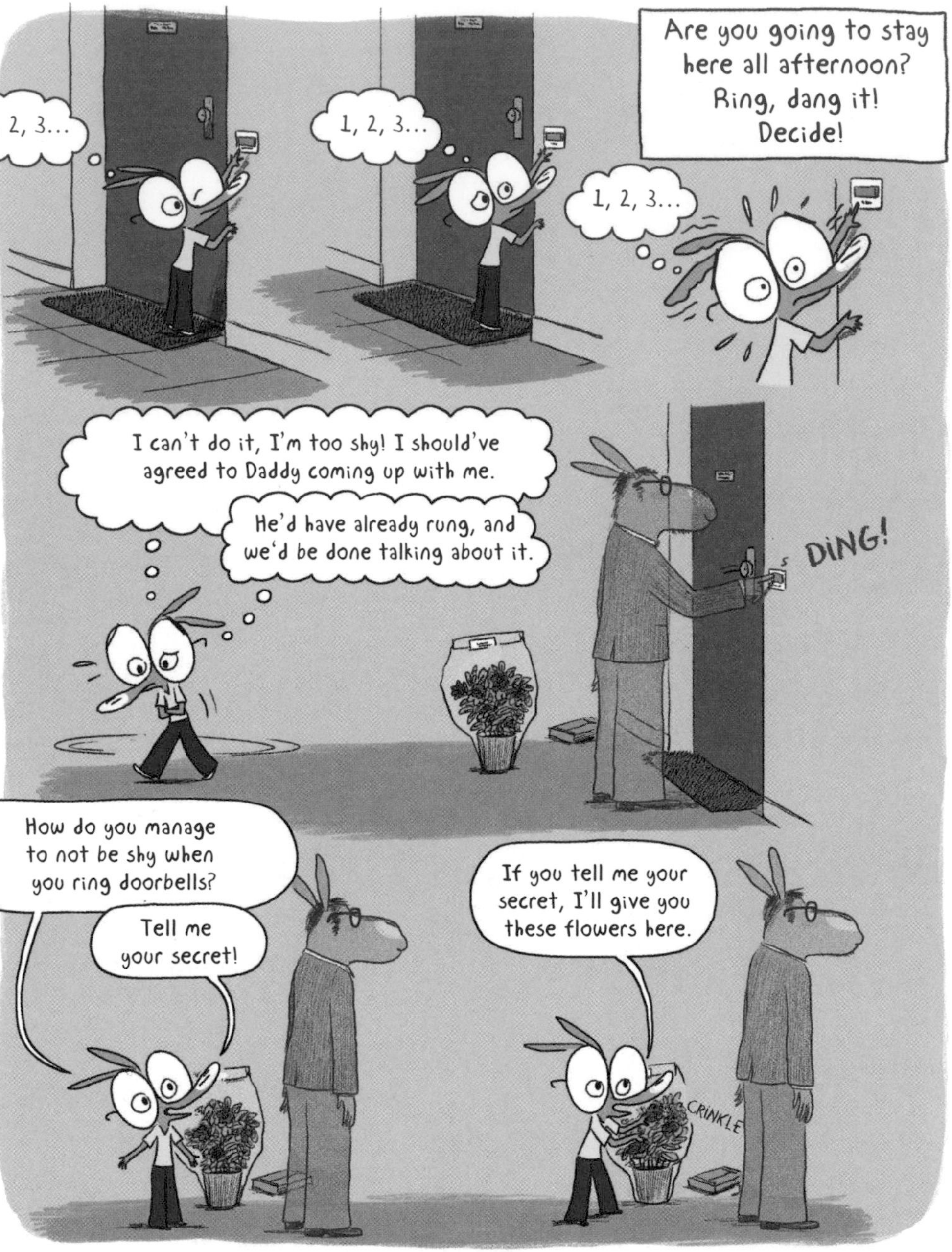
1, 2, 3...
1, 2, 3...
Are you going to stay here all afternoon? Ring, dang it! Decide!
1, 2, 3...
I can't do it, I'm too shy! I should've agreed to Daddy coming up with me.
He'd have already rung, and we'd be done talking about it.
DiNG!
How do you manage to not be shy when you ring doorbells?
Tell me your secret!
If you tell me your secret, I'll give you these flowers here.
CRINKLE

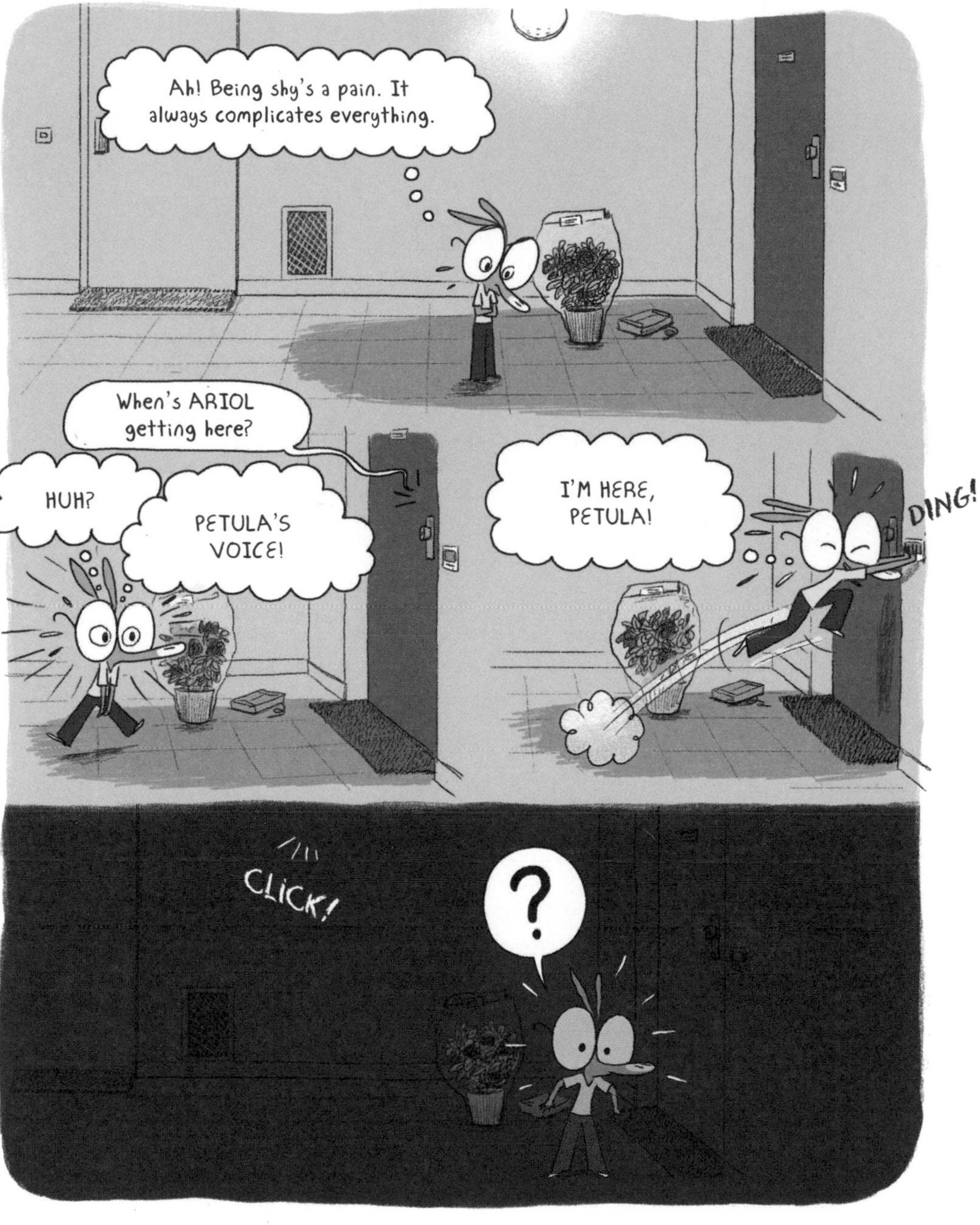
Ah! Being shy's a pain. It always complicates everything.
When's ARIOL getting here?
HUH?
PETULA'S VOICE!
I'M HERE, PETULA!
DING!
CLICK!
?

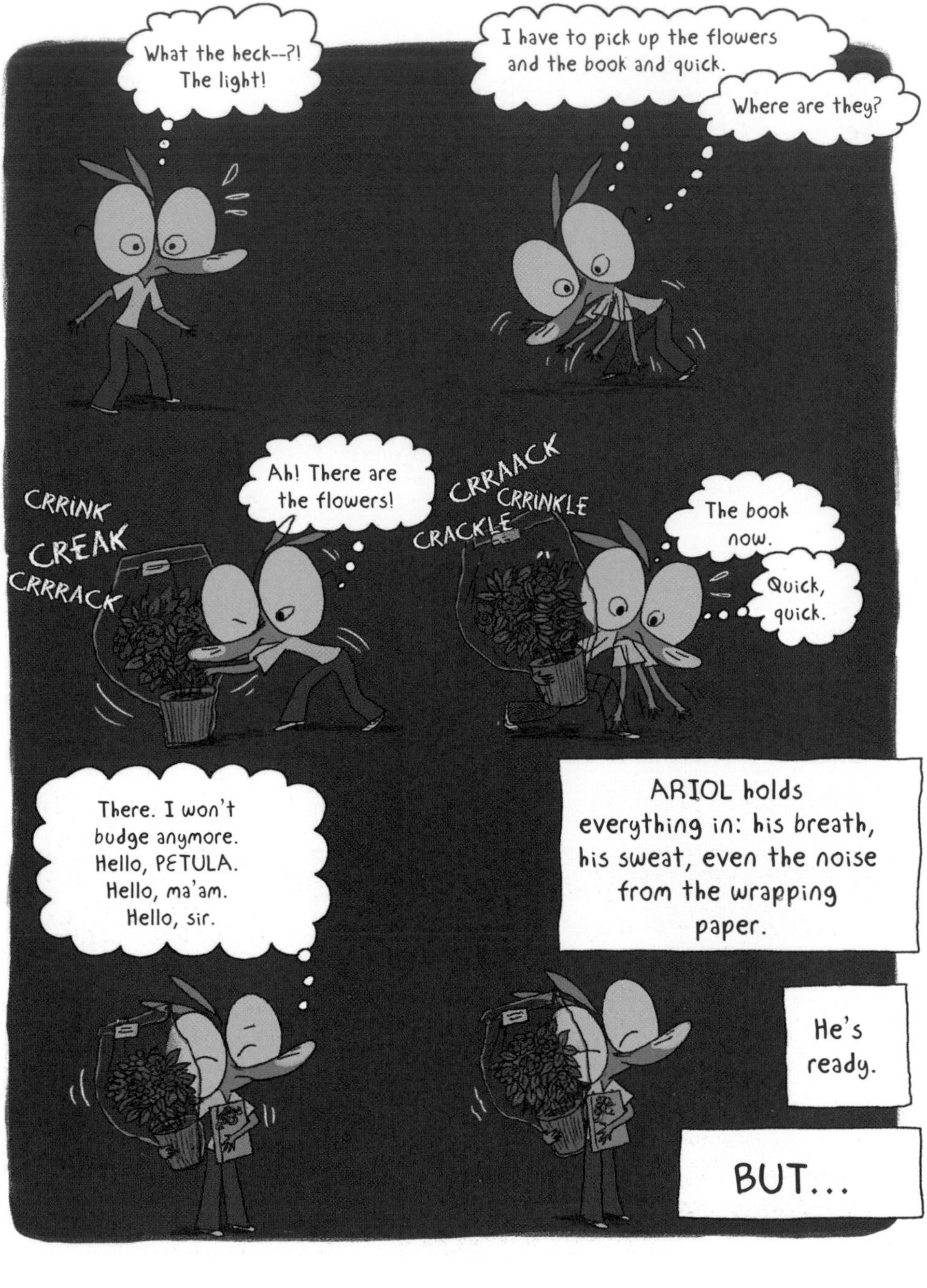
What the heck--?! The light!
I have to pick up the flowers and the book and quick.
Where are they?
CRRINK
CREAK
CRRRACK
Ah! There are the flowers!
CRRAACK
CRRINKLE
CRACKLE
The book now.
Quick, quick.
There. I won't budge anymore. Hello, PETULA. Hello, ma'am. Hello, sir.
ARIOL holds everything in: his breath, his sweat, even the noise from the wrapping paper.
He's ready.
BUT...

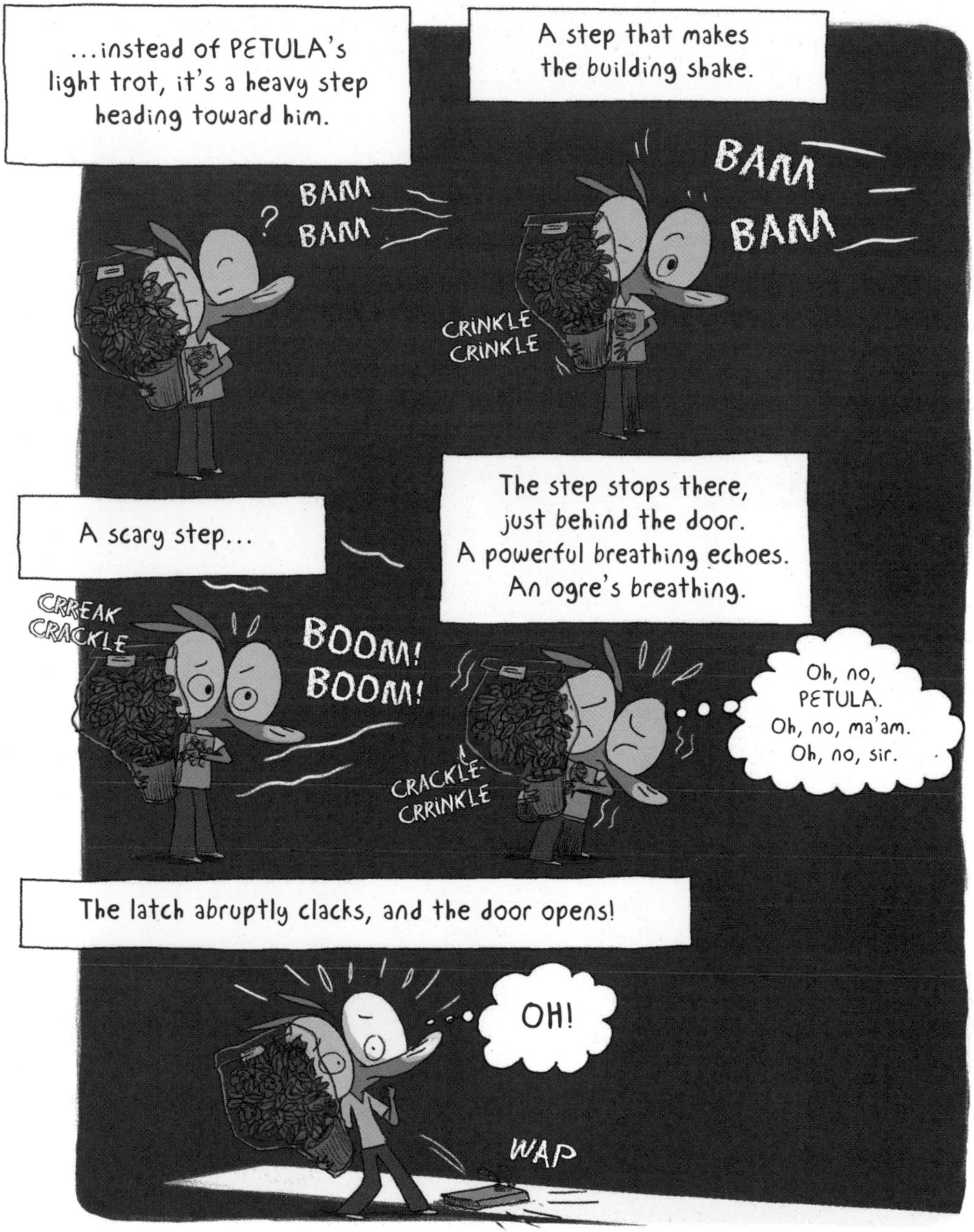
...instead of PETULA's light trot, it's a heavy step heading toward him.
A step that makes the building shake.
BAM BAM
?
BAM BAM
CRINKLE CRINKLE
A scary step...
CRREAK CRACKLE
BOOM! BOOM!
The step stops there, just behind the door. A powerful breathing echoes. An ogre's breathing.
CRACKLE CRRINKLE
Oh, no, PETULA. Oh, no, ma'am. Oh, no, sir.
The latch abruptly clacks, and the door opens!
OH!
WAP

CHAPTER 4

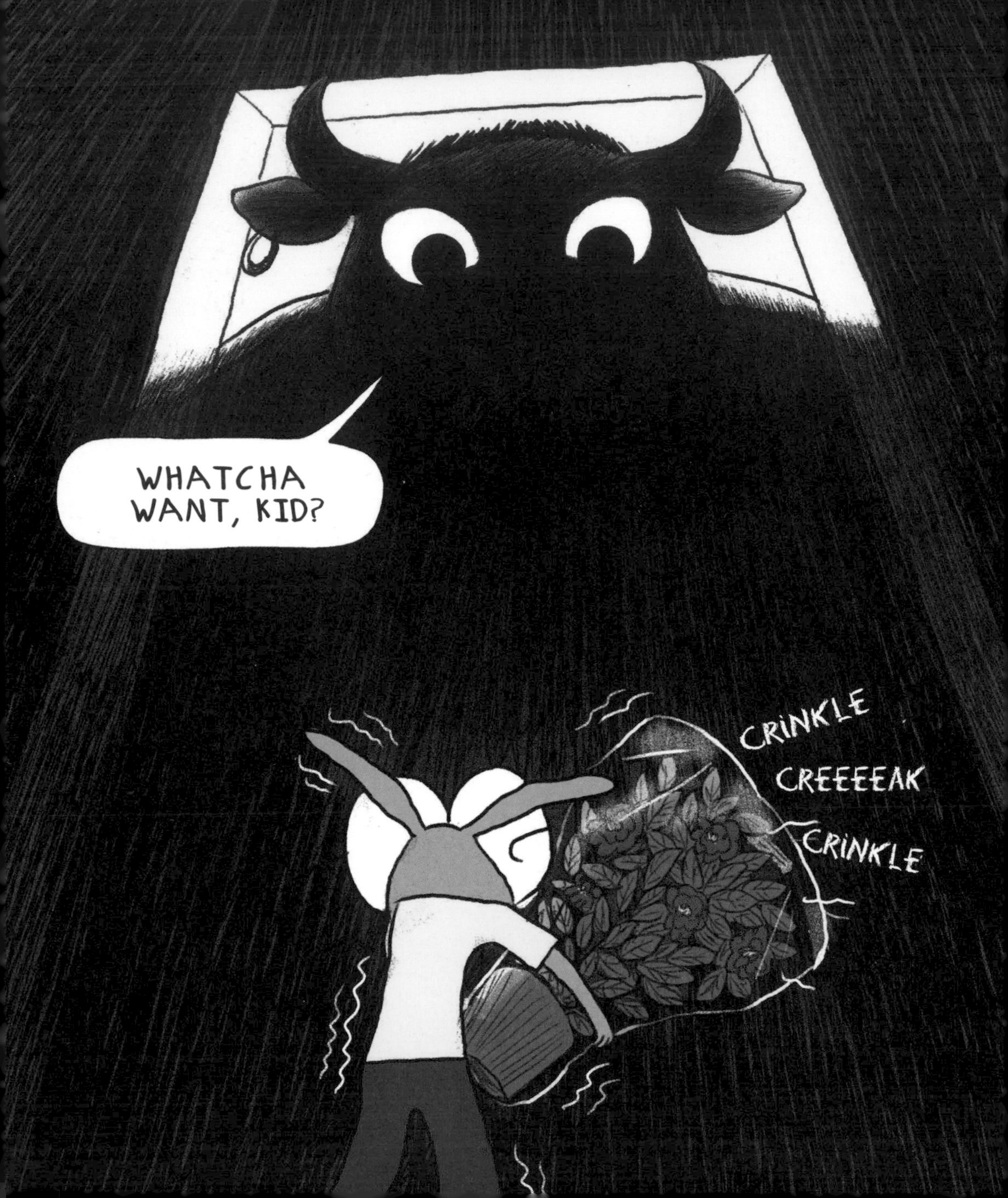
WHATCHA WANT, KID?
CRINKLE
CREEEEAK
CRINKLE

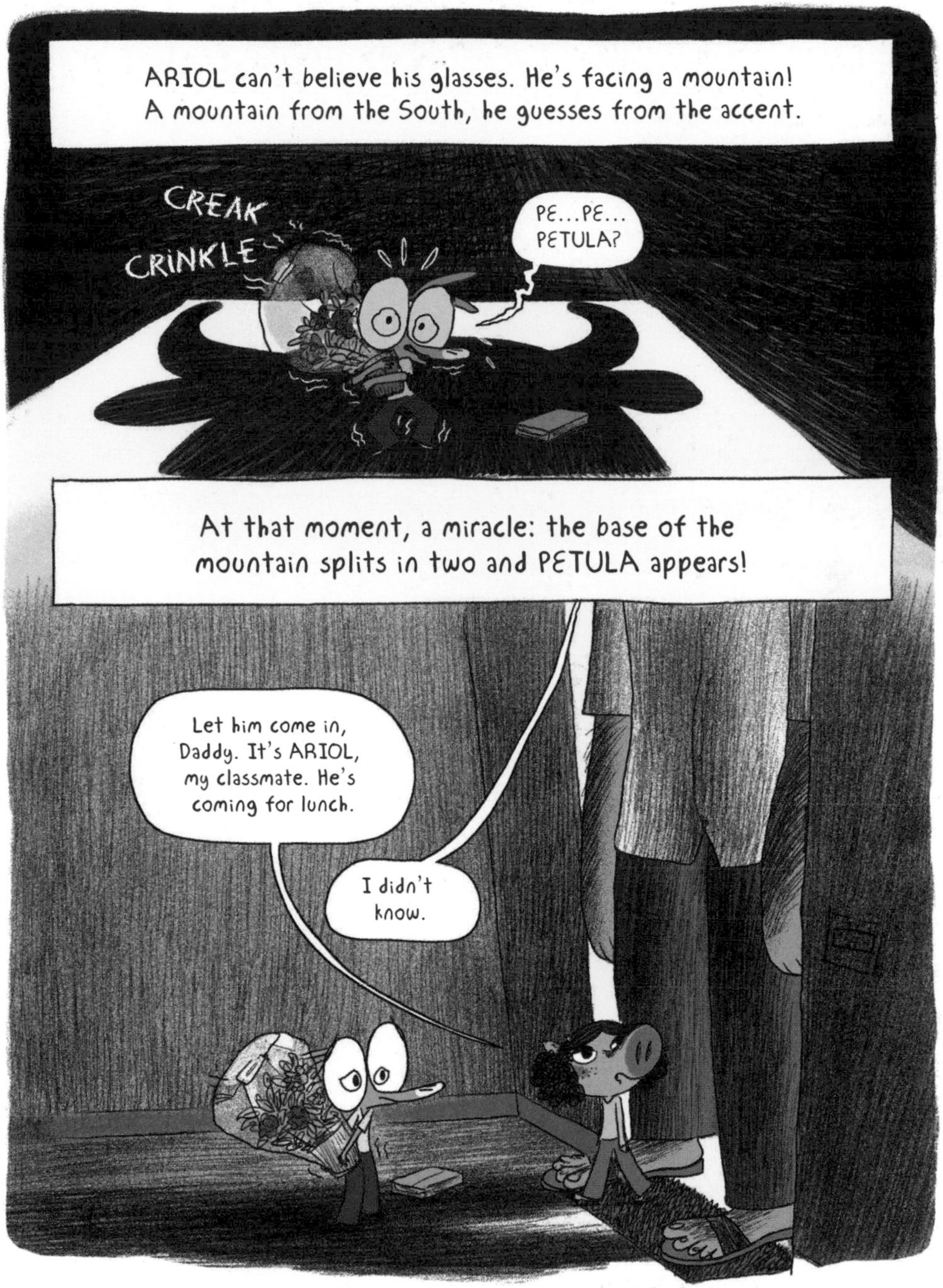
ARIOL can't believe his glasses. He's facing a mountain! A mountain from the South, he guesses from the accent.
CREAK
CRINKLE
PE...PE... PETULA?
At that moment, a miracle: the base of the mountain splits in two and PETULA appears!
Let him come in, Daddy. It's ARIOL, my classmate. He's coming for lunch.
I didn't know.

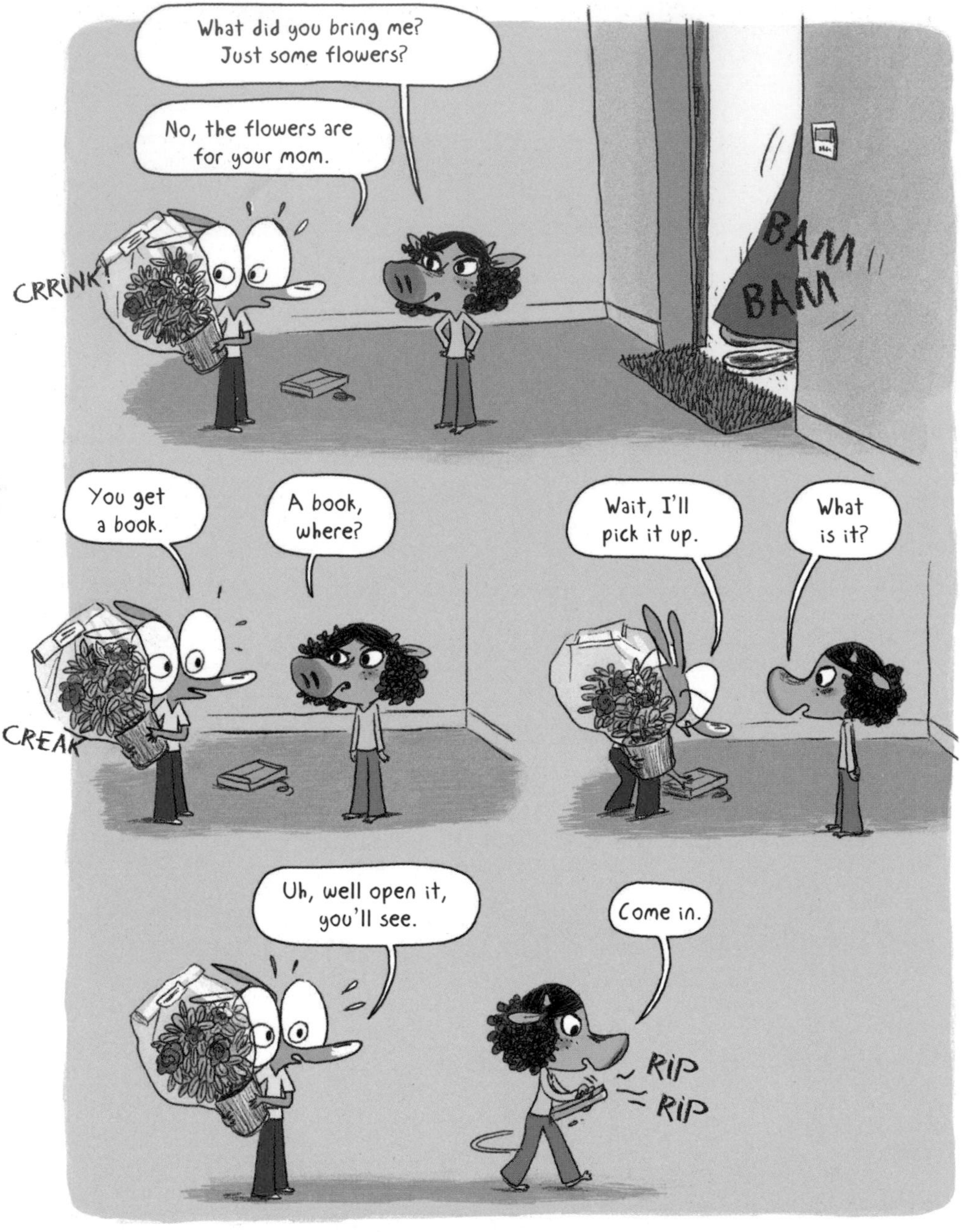
What did you bring me? Just some flowers?
No, the flowers are for your mom.
CRRINK!
BAM
BAM
You get a book.
A book, where?
CREAK
Wait, I'll pick it up.
What is it?
Uh, well open it, you'll see.
Come in.
RIP
RIP

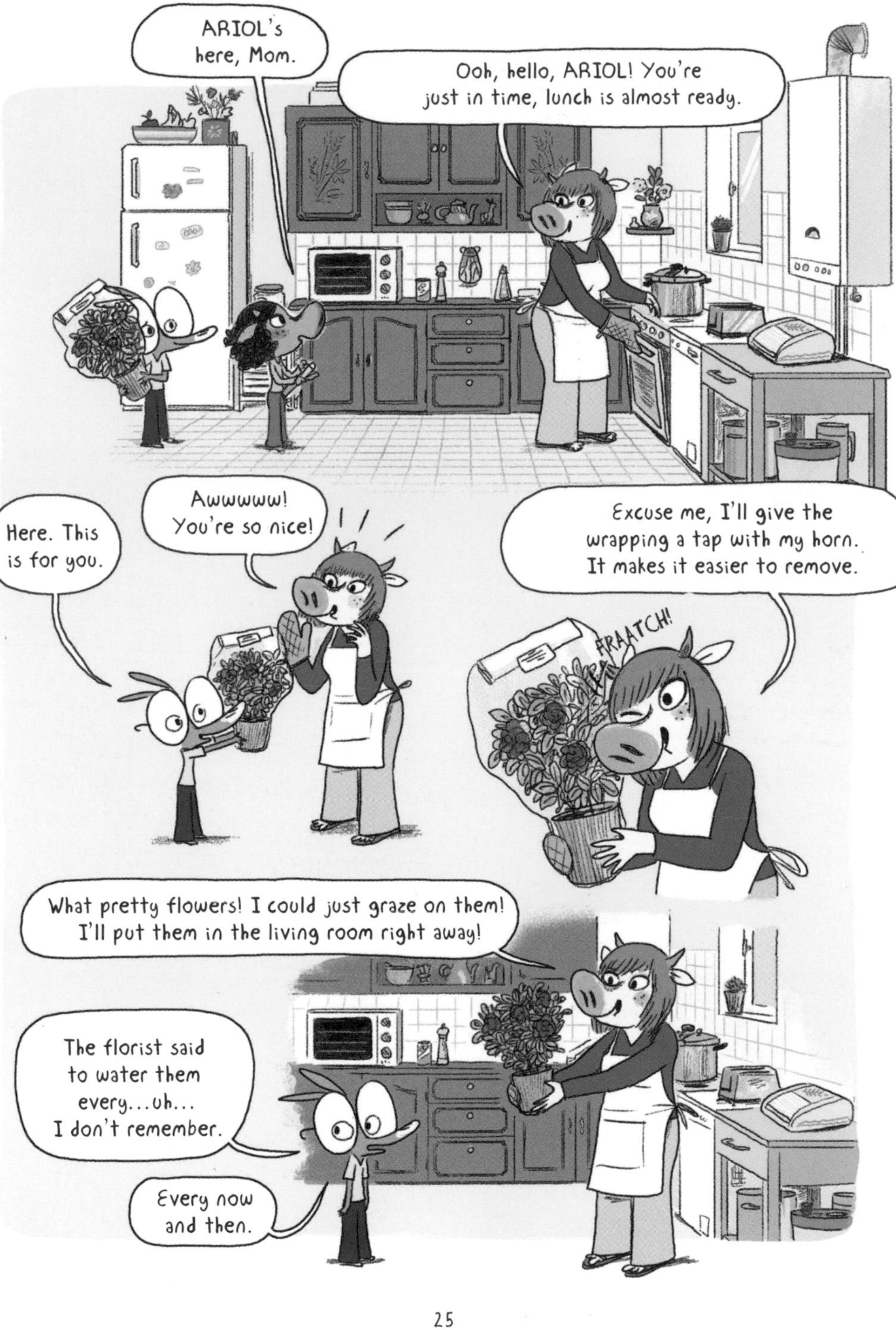
ARIOL's here, Mom.
Ooh, hello, ARIOL! You're just in time, lunch is almost ready.
Here. This is for you.
Awwwwww! You're so nice!
Excuse me, I'll give the wrapping a tap with my horn. It makes it easier to remove.
FRAATCH!
What pretty flowers! I could just graze on them! I'll put them in the living room right away!
The florist said to water them every...uh... I don't remember.
Every now and then.

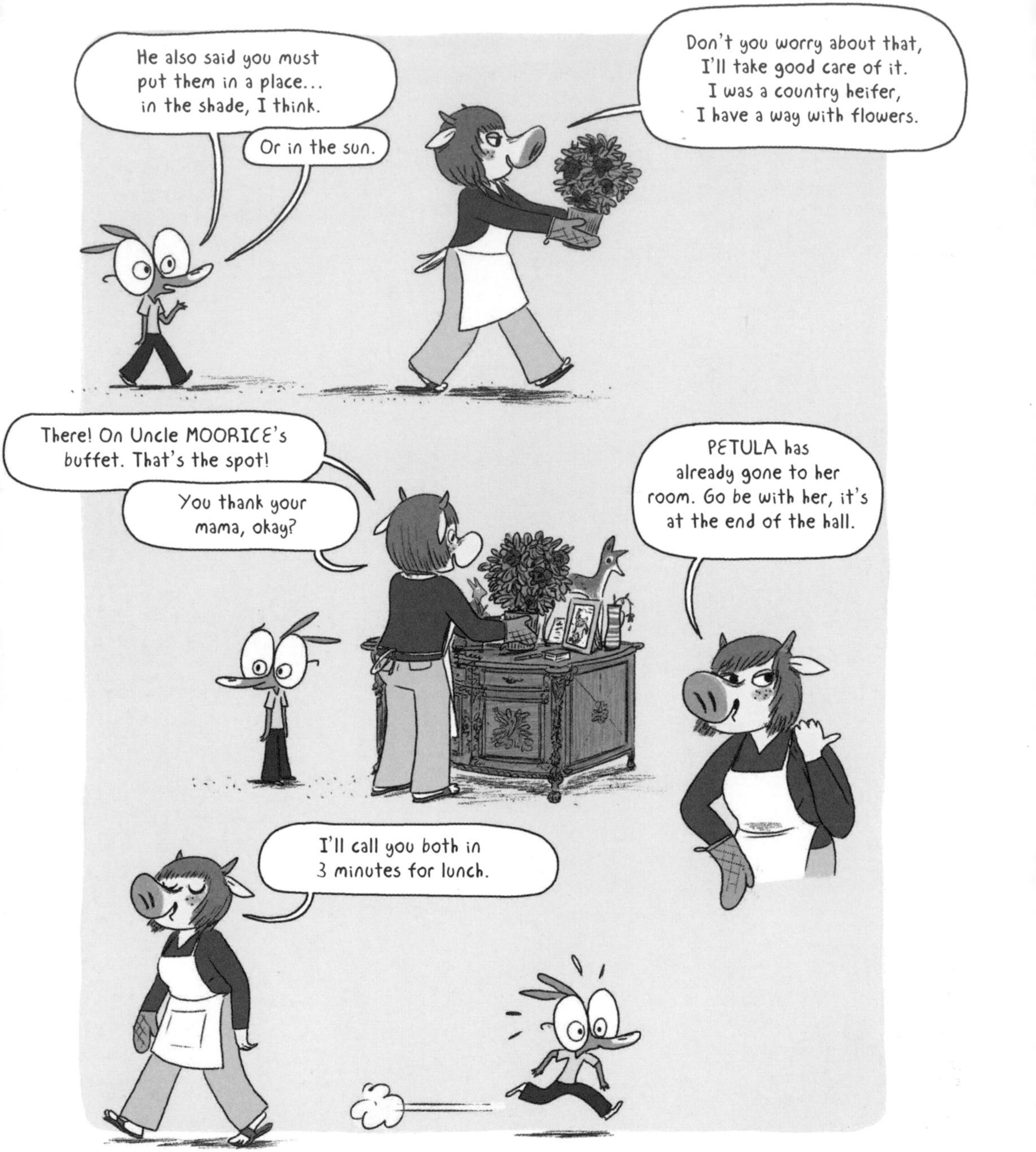
He also said you must put them in a place... in the shade, I think.
Or in the sun.
Don't you worry about that, I'll take good care of it. I was a country heifer, I have a way with flowers.
There! On Uncle MOORICE's buffet. That's the spot!
You thank your mama, okay?
PETULA has already gone to her room. Go be with her, it's at the end of the hall.
I'll call you both in 3 minutes for lunch.

CHAPTER 5

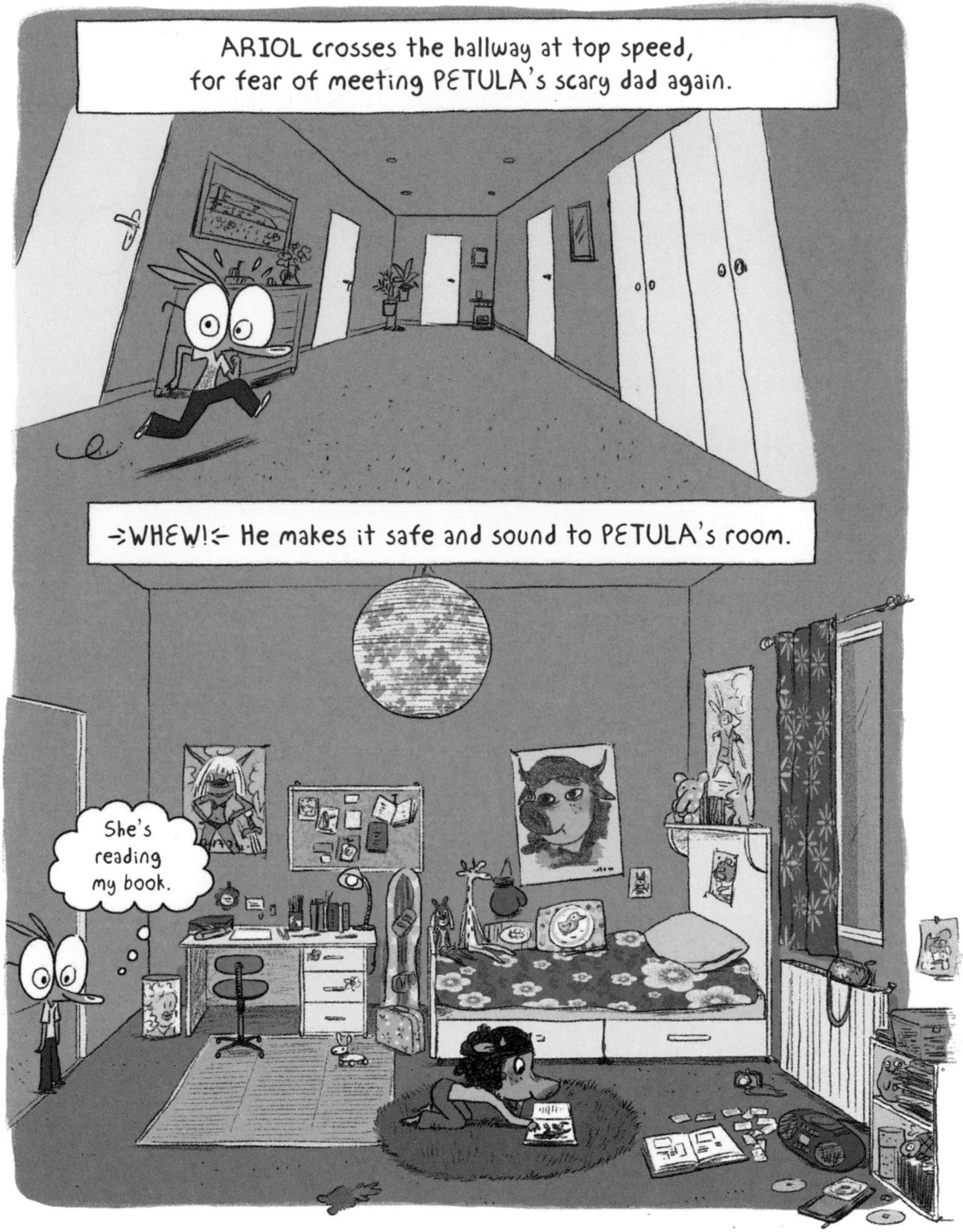
ARIOL crosses the hallway at top speed, for fear of meeting PETULA's scary dad again.
→WHEW!← He makes it safe and sound to PETULA's room.
She's reading my book.

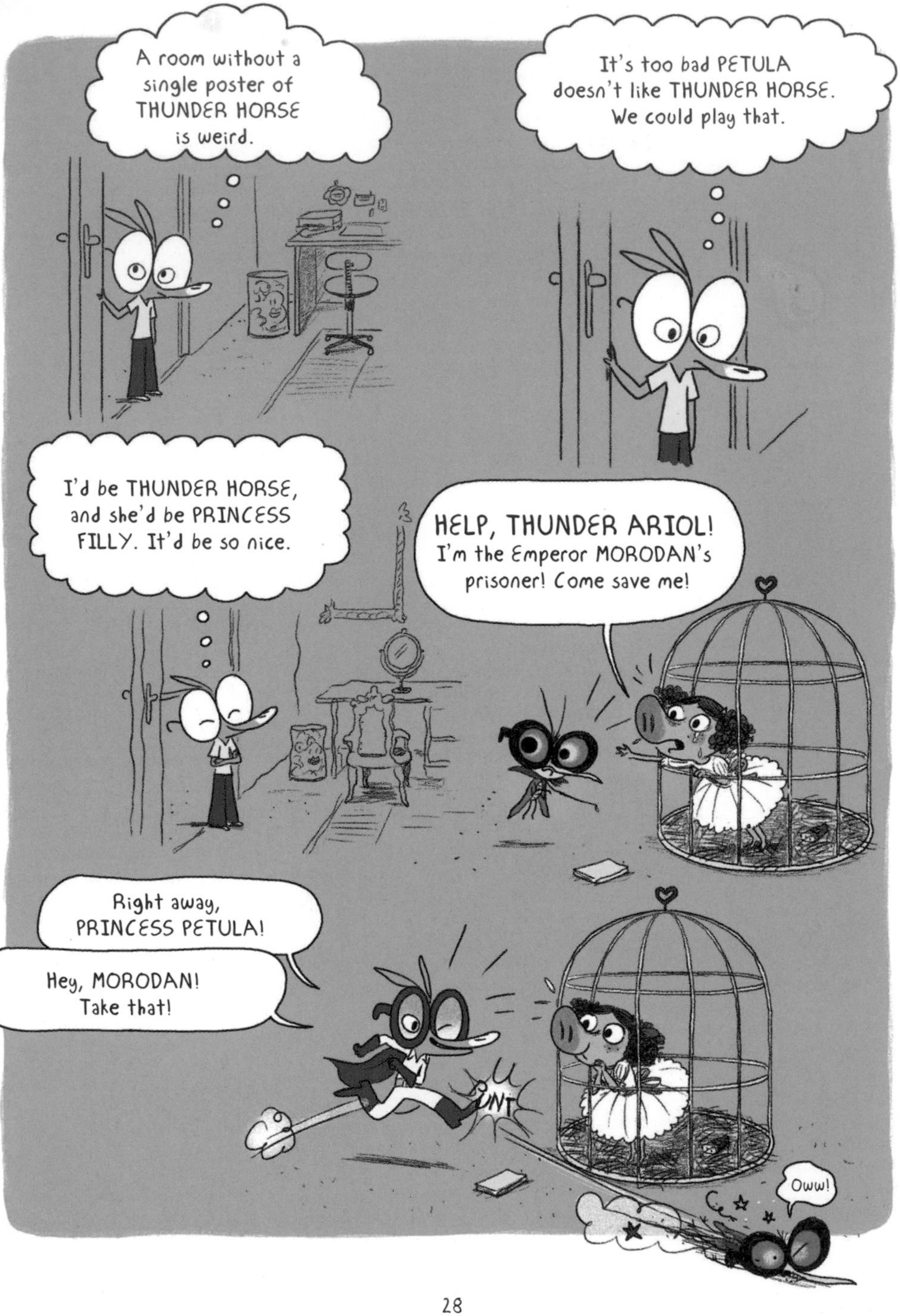
A room without a single poster of THUNDER HORSE is weird.
It's too bad PETULA doesn't like THUNDER HORSE. We could play that.
I'd be THUNDER HORSE, and she'd be PRINCESS FILLY. It'd be so nice.
HELP, THUNDER ARIOL! I'm the Emperor MORODAN's prisoner! Come save me!
Right away, PRINCESS PETULA!
Hey, MORODAN! Take that!
Oww!

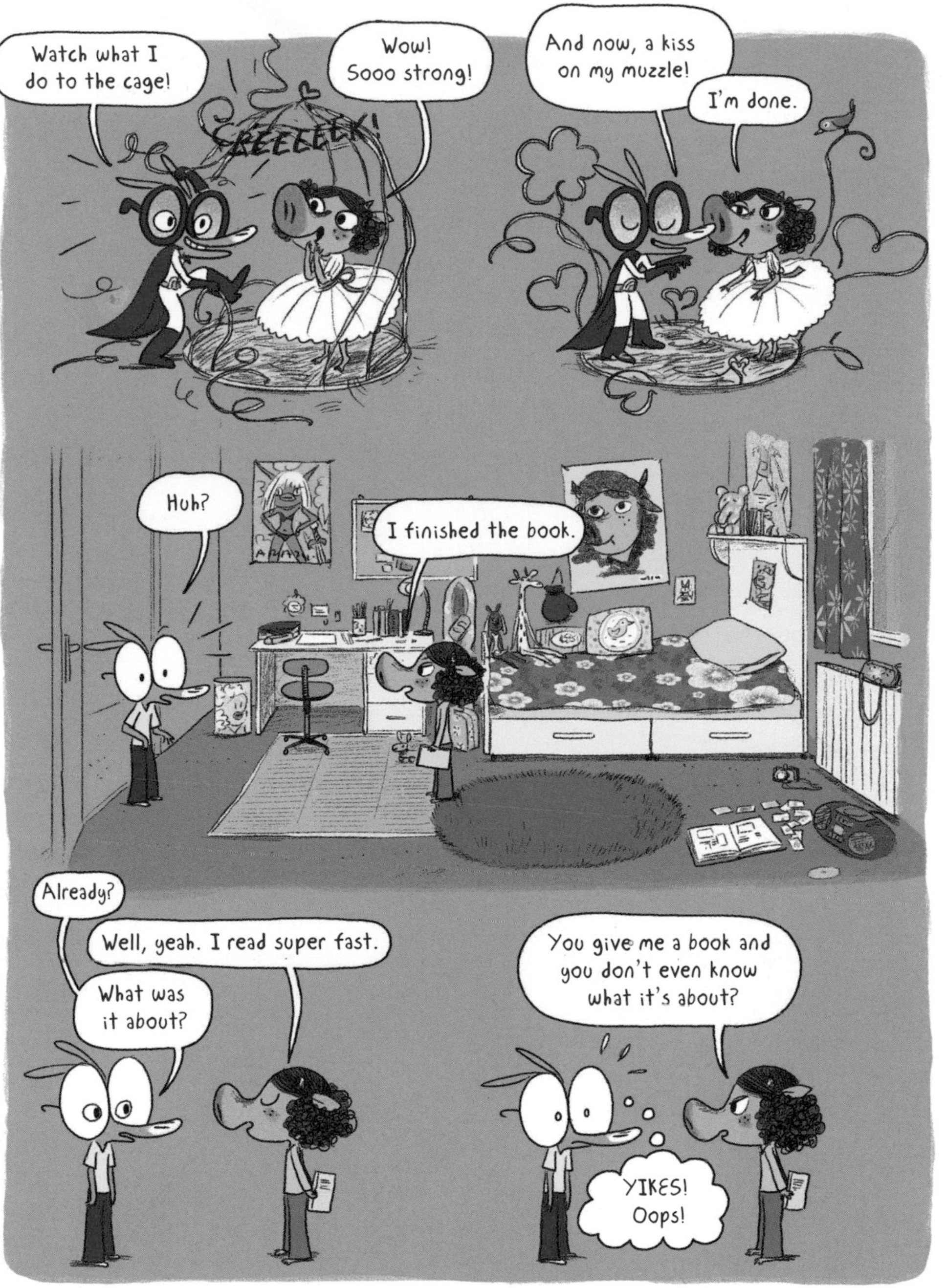
Watch what I do to the cage!
CREEEEEK!
Wow! Sooo strong!
And now, a kiss on my muzzle!
I'm done.
Huh?
I finished the book.
Already?
Well, yeah. I read super fast.
What was it about?
You give me a book and you don't even know what it's about?
YIKES! Oops!

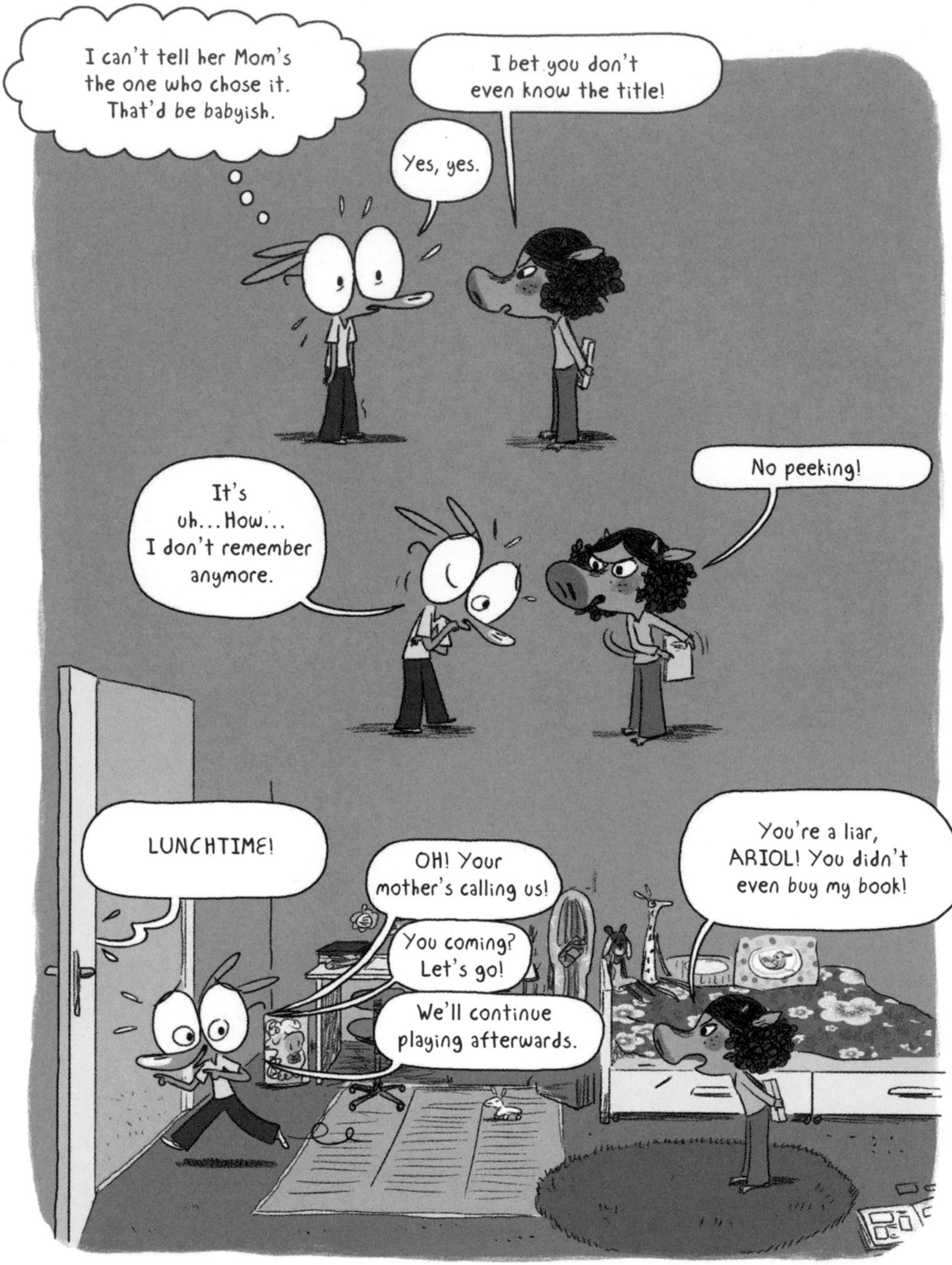
I can't tell her Mom's the one who chose it. That'd be babyish.
I bet you don't even know the title!
Yes, yes.
It's uh... How... I don't remember anymore.
No peeking!
LUNCHTIME!
OH! Your mother's calling us!
You coming? Let's go!
We'll continue playing afterwards.
You're a liar, ARIOL! You didn't even buy my book!

CHAPTER 6

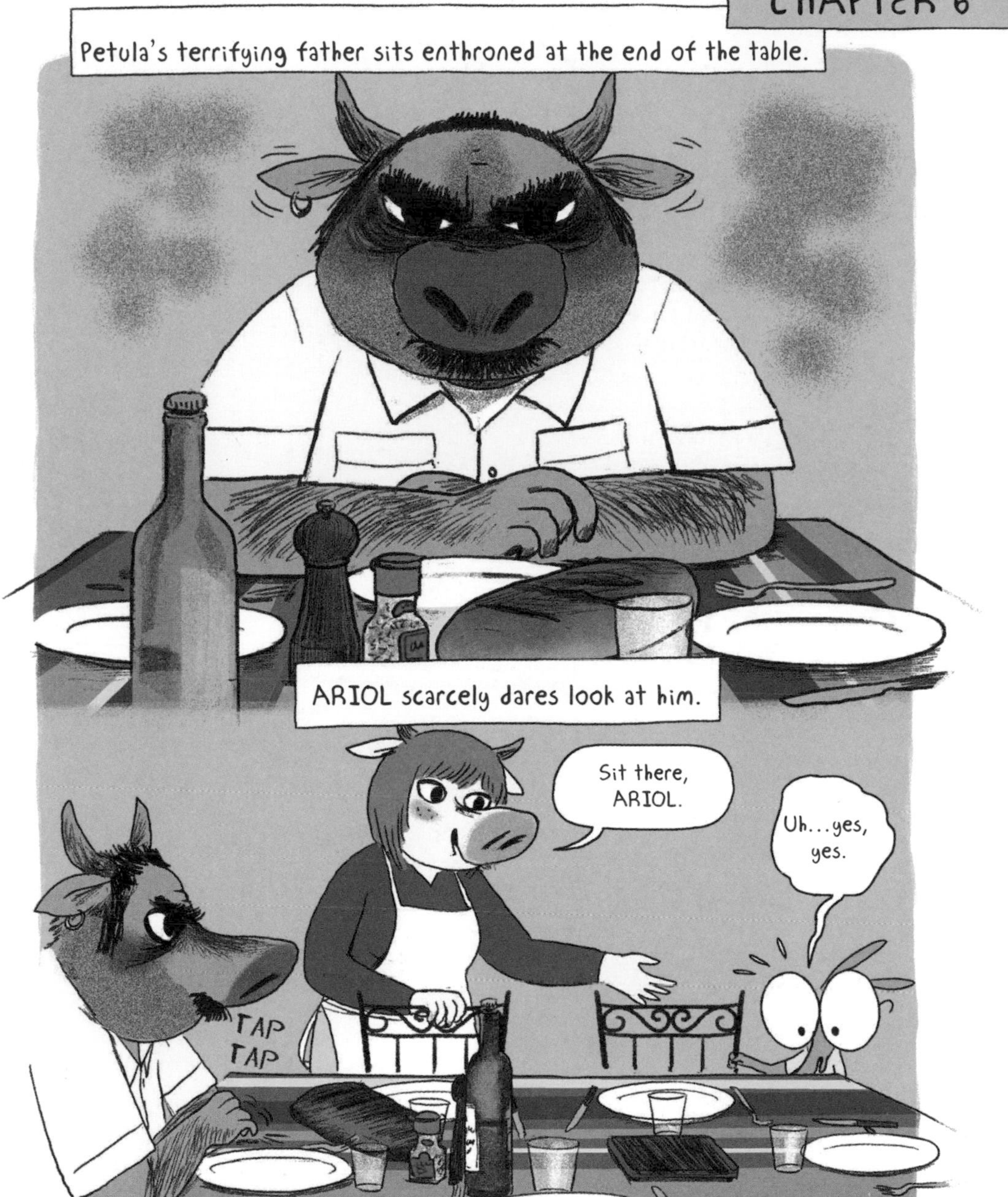

Petula's terrifying father sits enthroned at the end of the table.
ARIOL scarcely dares look at him.
Sit there, ARIOL.
Uh...yes, yes.
TAP TAP

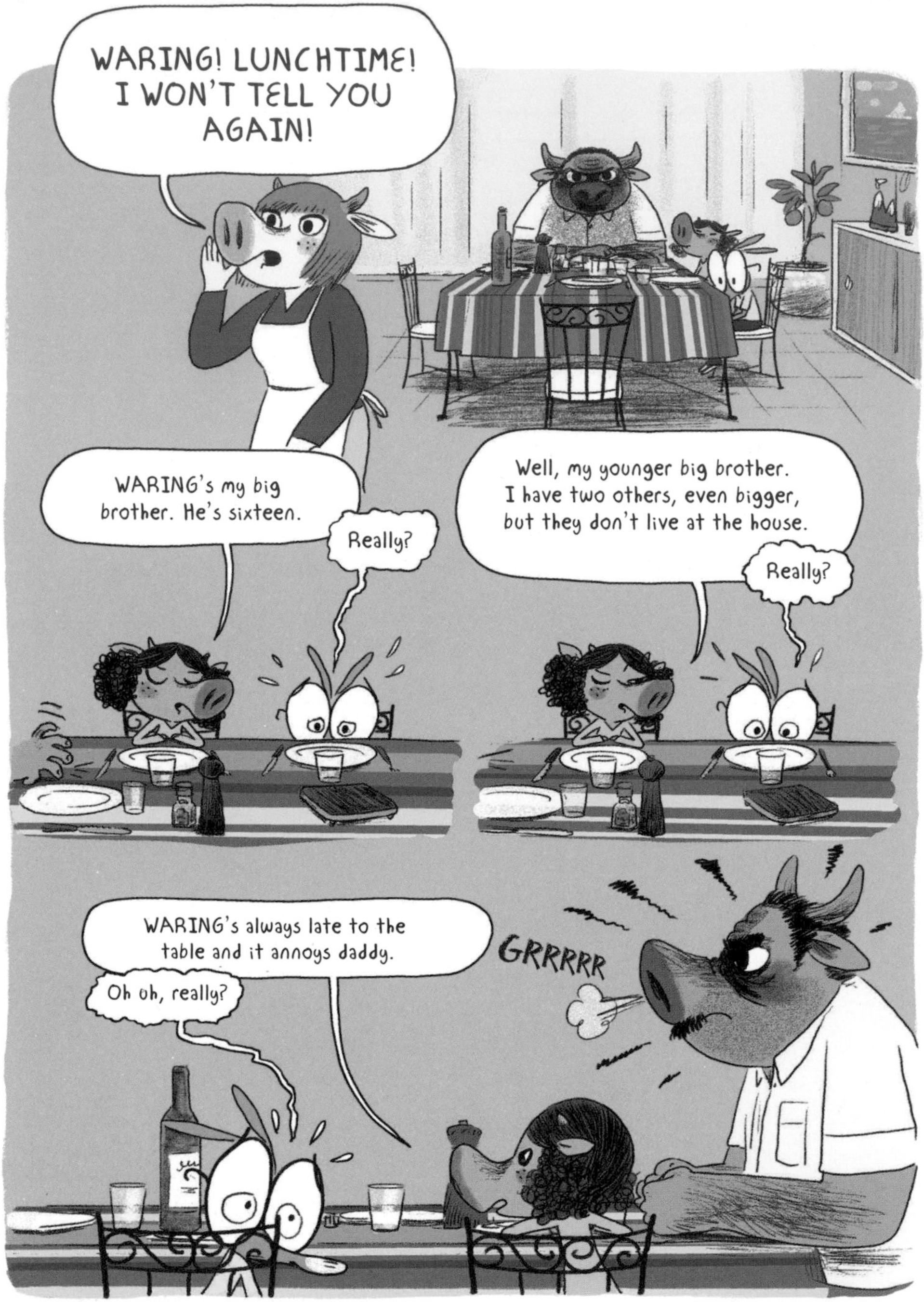
WARING! LUNCHTIME! I WON'T TELL YOU AGAIN!
WARING's my big brother. He's sixteen.
Really?
Well, my younger big brother. I have two others, even bigger, but they don't live at the house.
Really?
WARING's always late to the table and it annoys daddy.
Oh oh, really?
GRRRRR

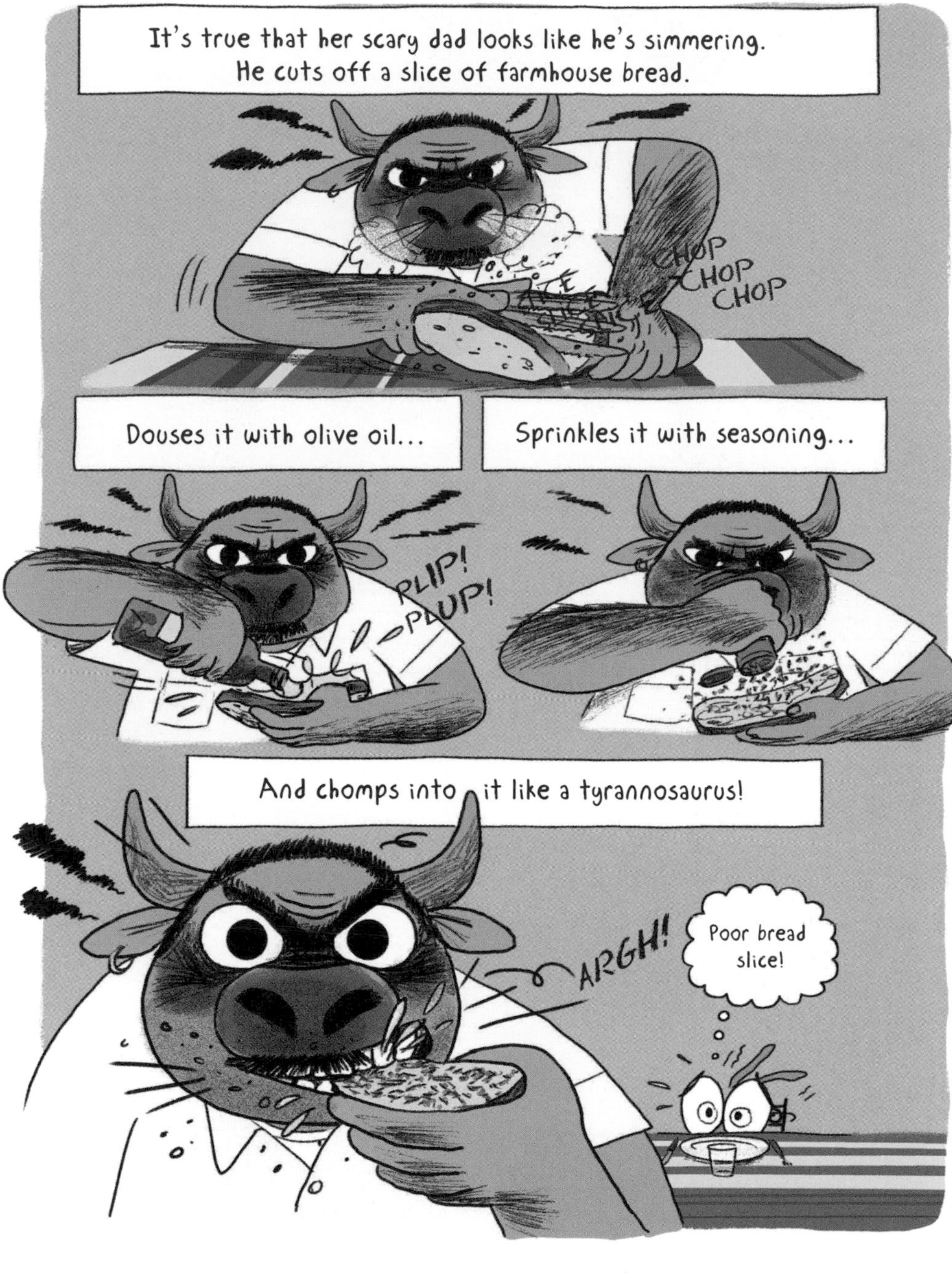
It's true that her scary dad looks like he's simmering.
He cuts off a slice of farmhouse bread.
CHOP
CHOP
CHOP
Douses it with olive oil...
PLIP!
PLUP!
Sprinkles it with seasoning...
And chomps into it like a tyrannosaurus!
ARGH!
Poor bread slice!

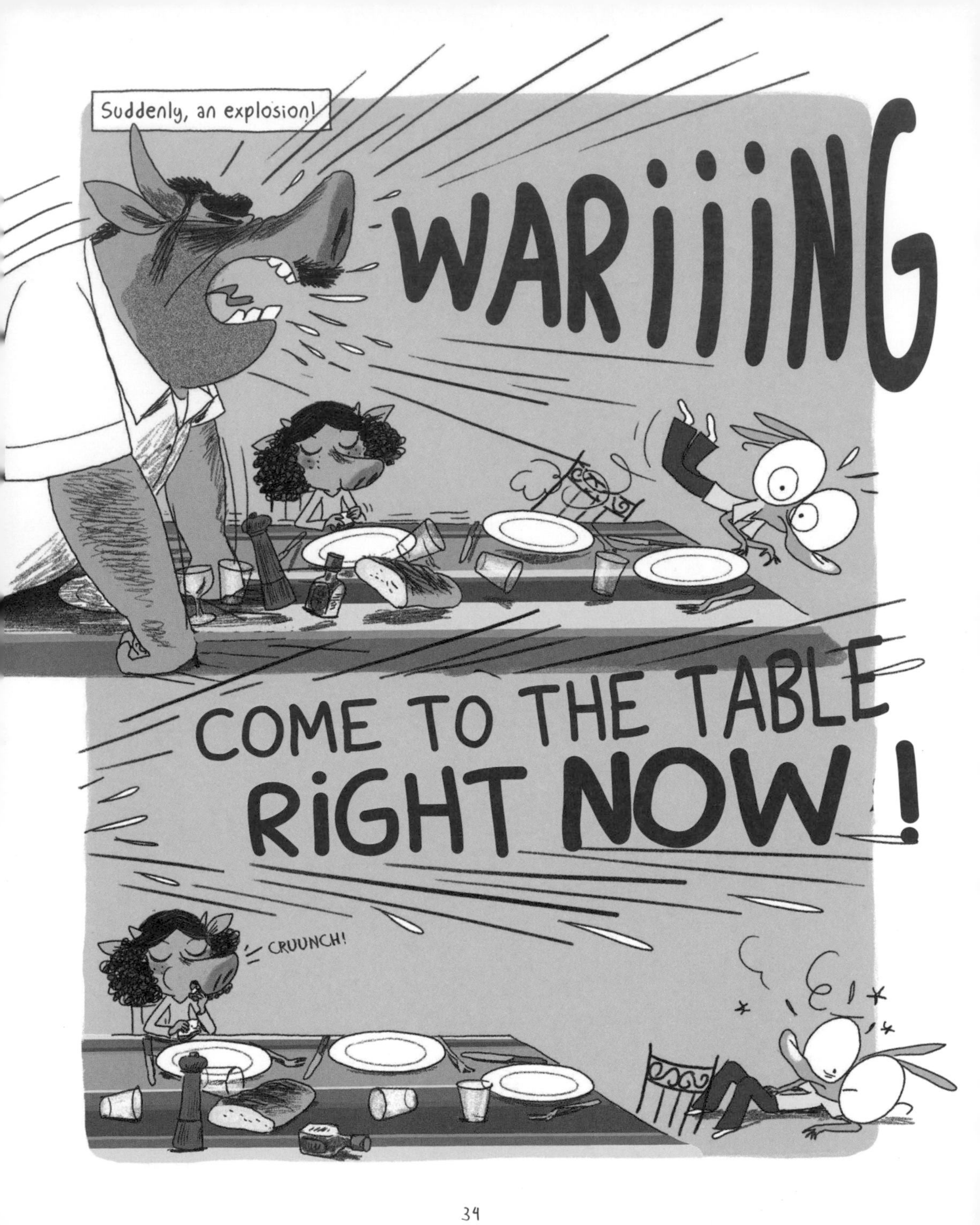
Suddenly, an explosion!
WARiiiNG
COME TO THE TABLE
RiGHT NOW!
CRUUNCH!

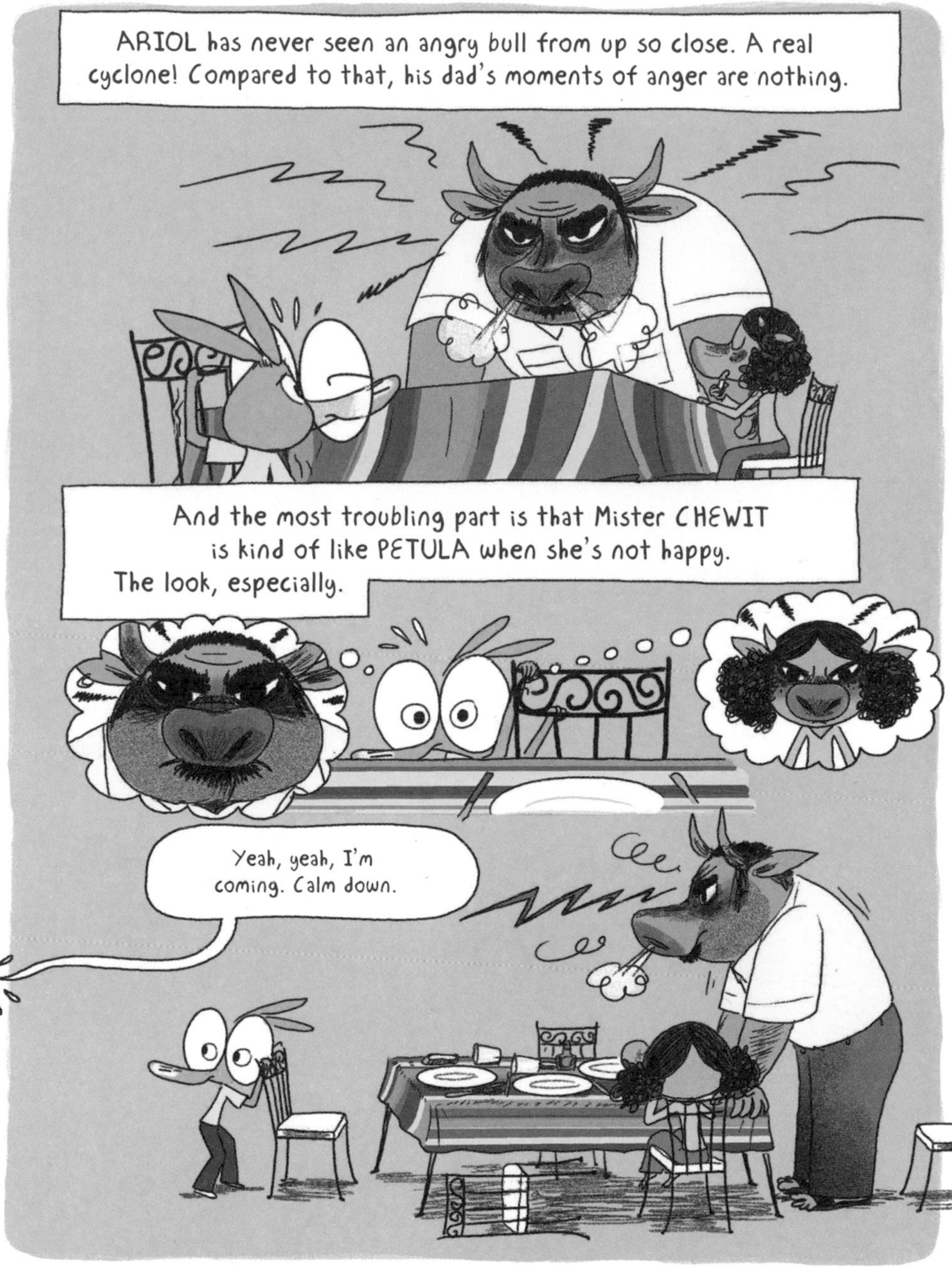
ARIOL has never seen an angry bull from up so close. A real cyclone! Compared to that, his dad's moments of anger are nothing.
And the most troubling part is that Mister CHEWIT is kind of like PETULA when she's not happy. The look, especially.
Yeah, yeah, I'm coming. Calm down.

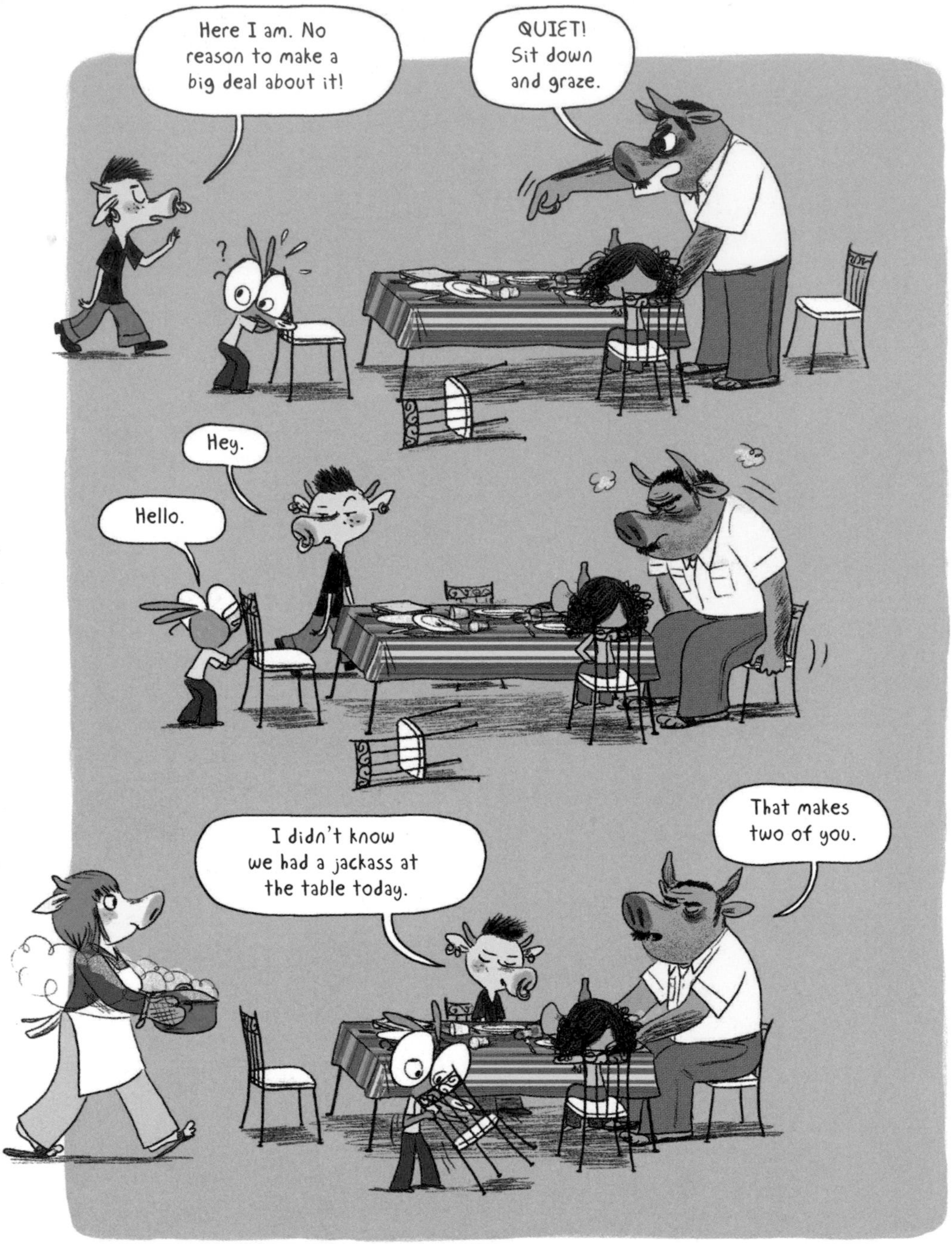
Here I am. No reason to make a big deal about it!
QUIET! Sit down and graze.
Hey.
Hello.
I didn't know we had a jackass at the table today.
That makes two of you.

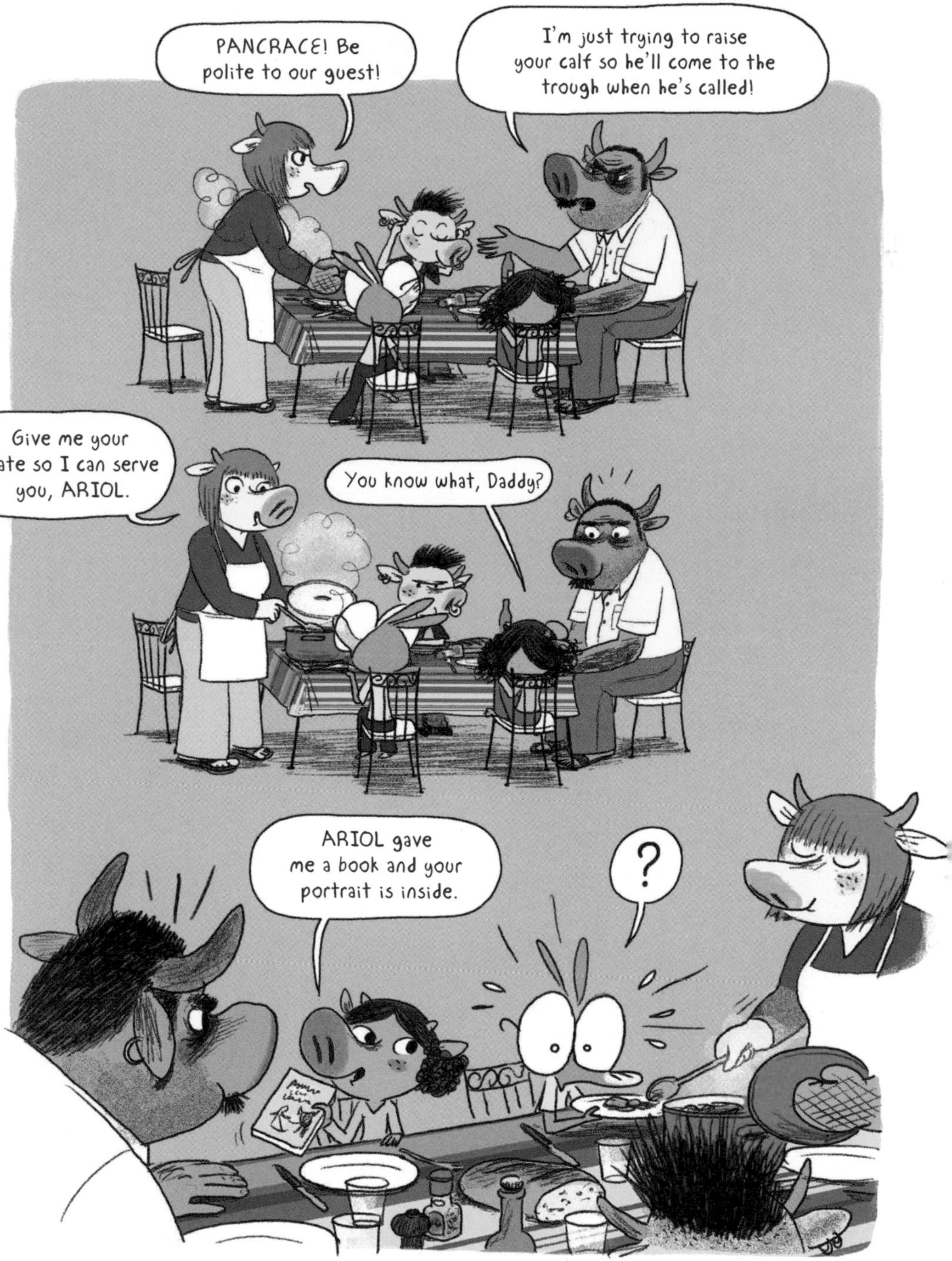
PANCRACE! Be polite to our guest!
I'm just trying to raise your calf so he'll come to the trough when he's called!
Give me your plate so I can serve you, ARIOL.
You know what, Daddy?
ARIOL gave me a book and your portrait is inside.
?

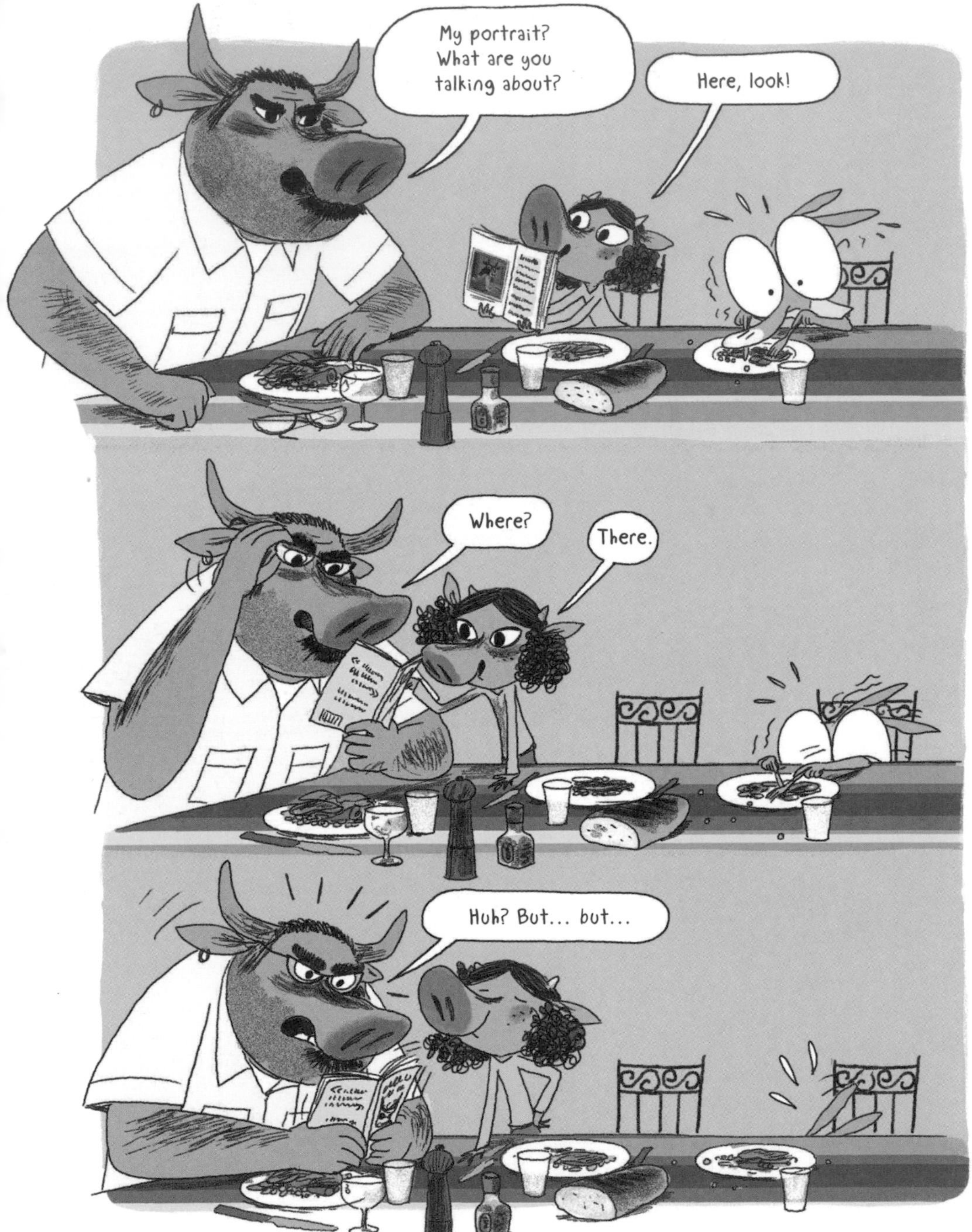

My portrait? What are you talking about?
Here, look!
Where?
There.
Huh? But... but...

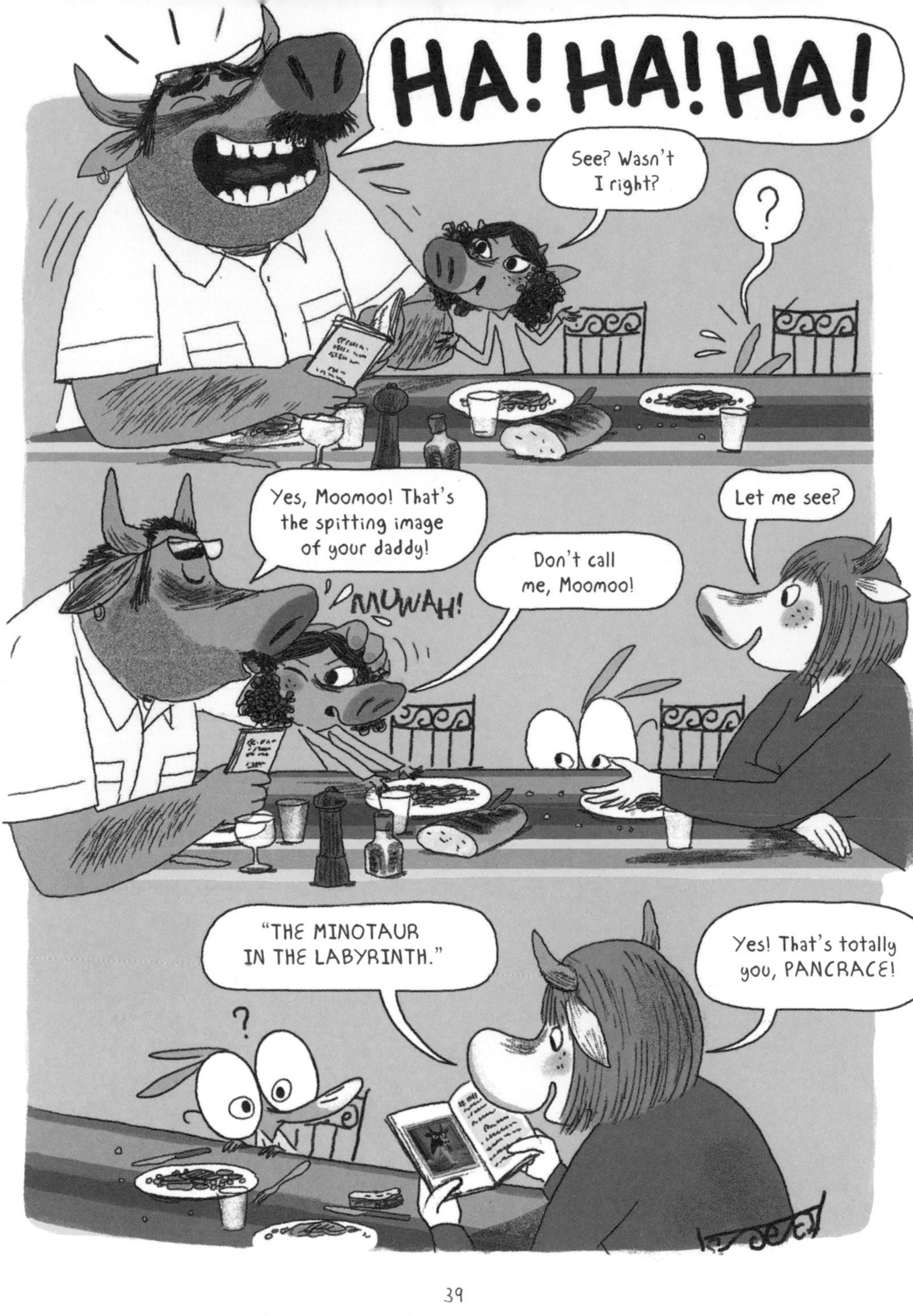
HA! HA! HA!
See? Wasn't I right?
?
Yes, Moomoo! That's the spitting image of your daddy!
MUWAH!
Let me see?
Don't call me, Moomoo!
"THE MINOTAUR IN THE LABYRINTH."
Yes! That's totally you, PANCRACE!
?

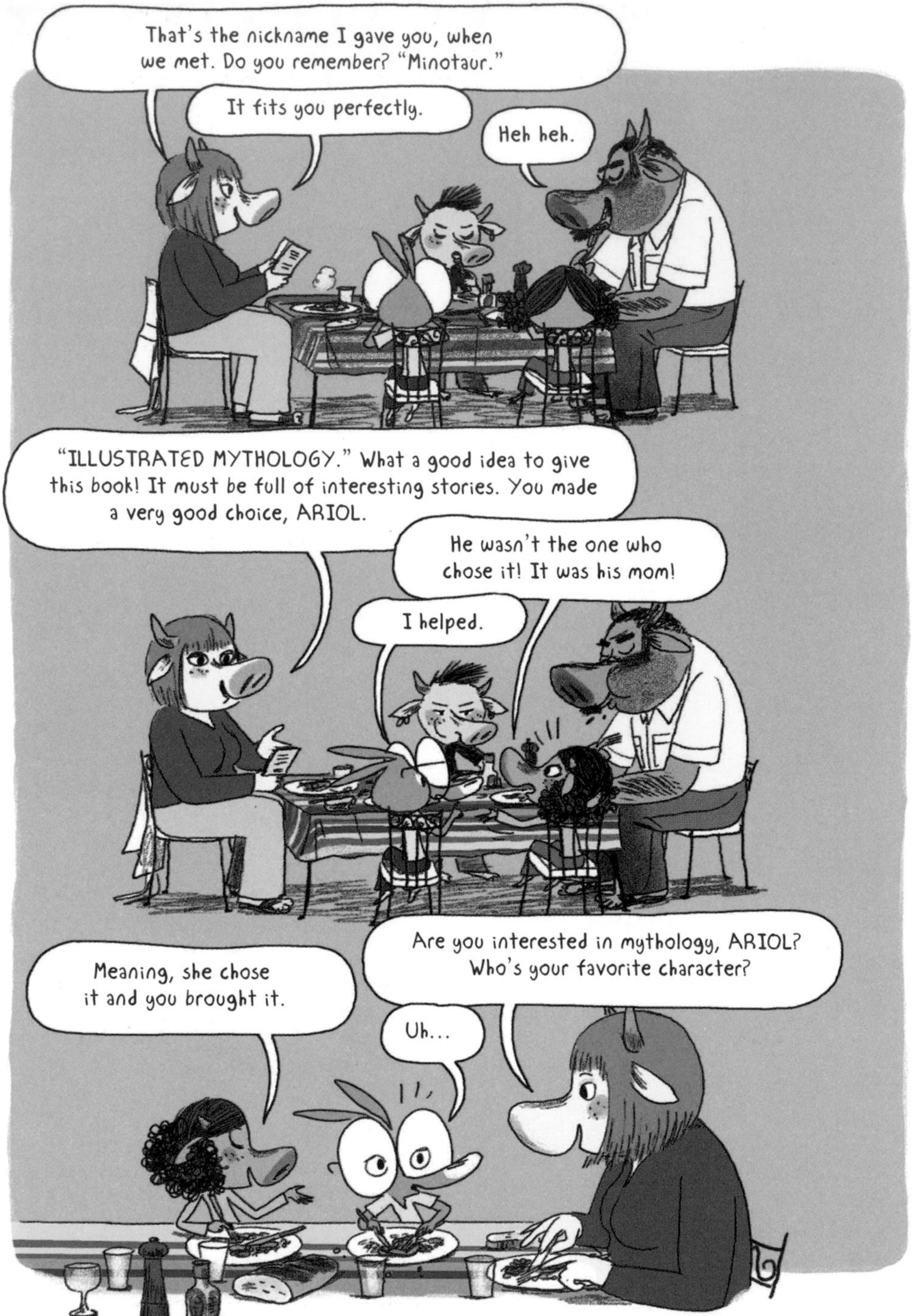
That's the nickname I gave you, when we met. Do you remember? "Minotaur."
It fits you perfectly.
Heh heh.
"ILLUSTRATED MYTHOLOGY." What a good idea to give this book! It must be full of interesting stories. You made a very good choice, ARIOL.
He wasn't the one who chose it! It was his mom!
I helped.
Meaning, she chose it and you brought it.
Are you interested in mythology, ARIOL? Who's your favorite character?
Uh...

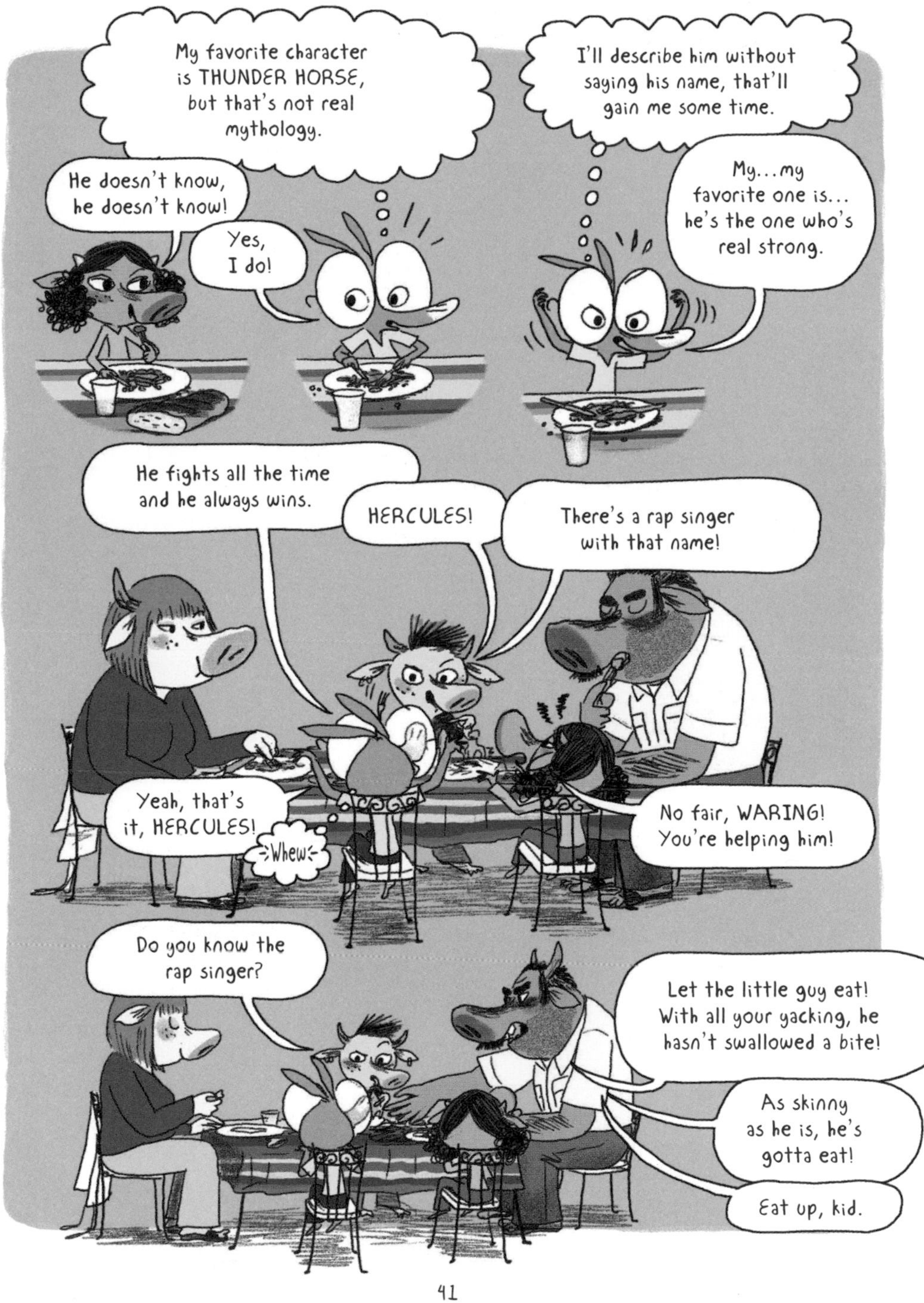
My favorite character is THUNDER HORSE, but that's not real mythology.
He doesn't know, he doesn't know!
Yes, I do!
I'll describe him without saying his name, that'll gain me some time.
My...my favorite one is... he's the one who's real strong.
He fights all the time and he always wins.
HERCULES!
There's a rap singer with that name!
Yeah, that's it, HERCULES!
Whew
No fair, WARING! You're helping him!
Do you know the rap singer?
Let the little guy eat! With all your yacking, he hasn't swallowed a bite!
As skinny as he is, he's gotta eat!
Eat up, kid.

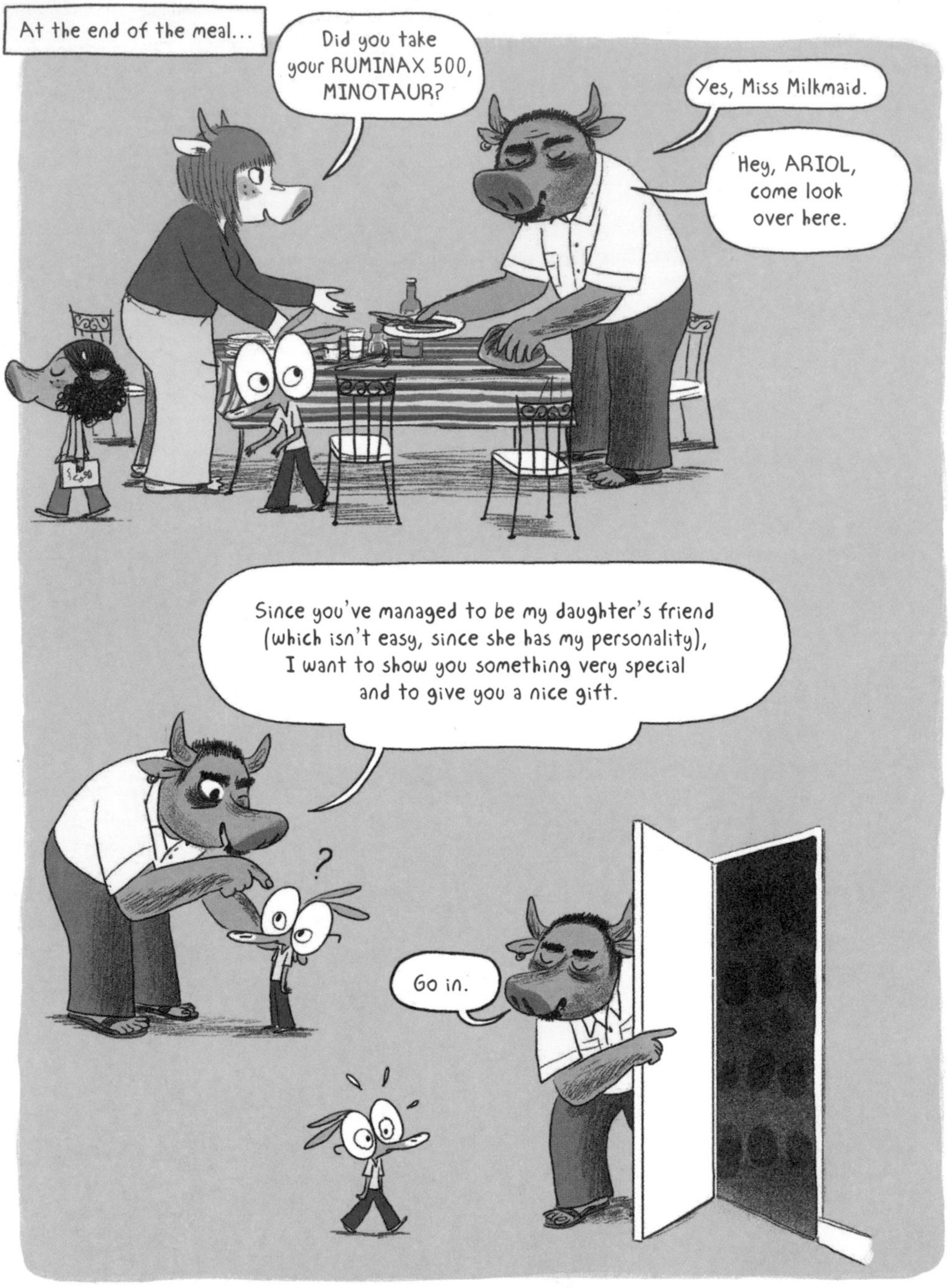
At the end of the meal...
Did you take your RUMINAX 500, MINOTAUR?
Yes, Miss Milkmaid.
Hey, ARIOL, come look over here.
Since you've managed to be my daughter's friend (which isn't easy, since she has my personality), I want to show you something very special and to give you a nice gift.
?
Go in.

CHAPTER 7

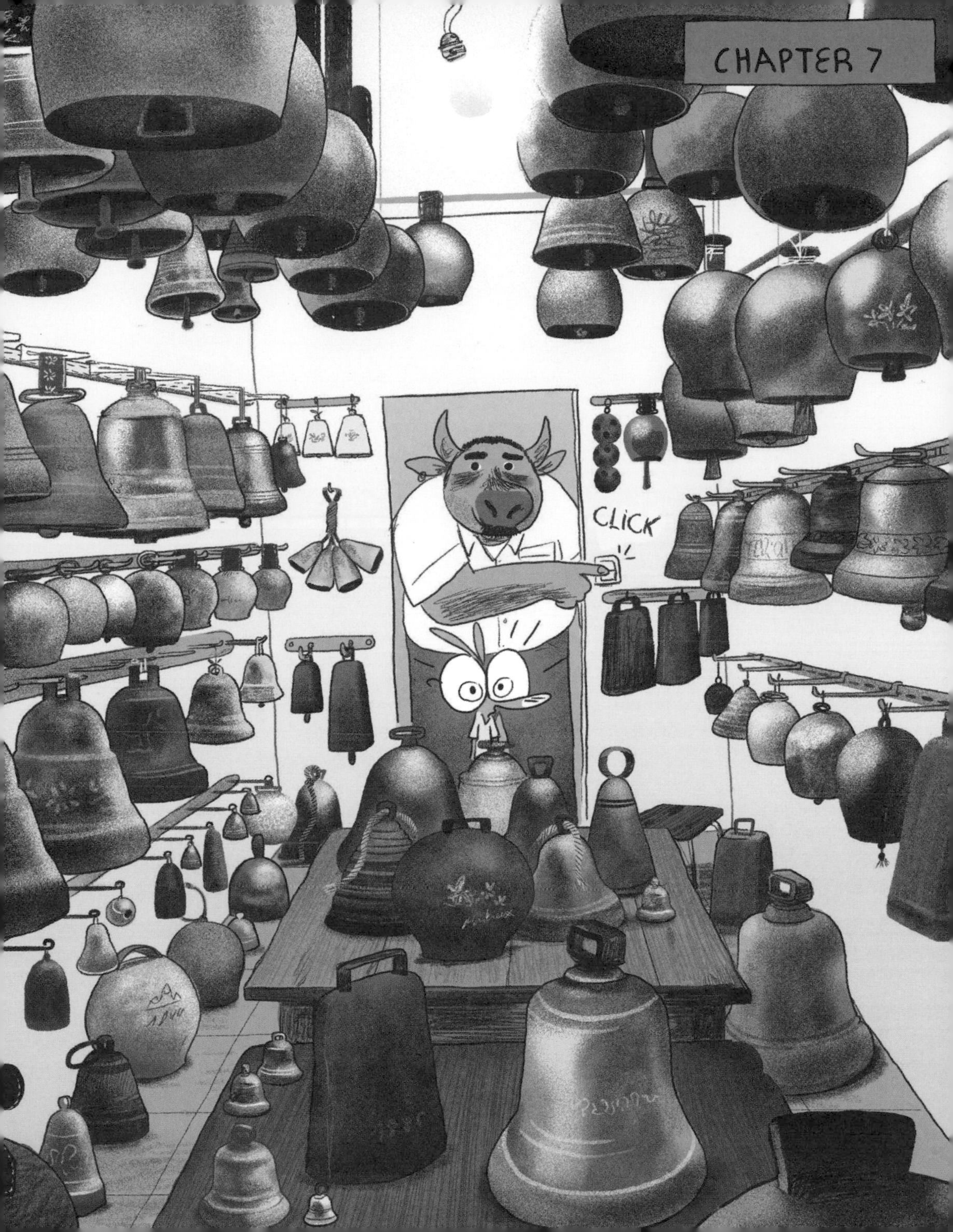
CLICK

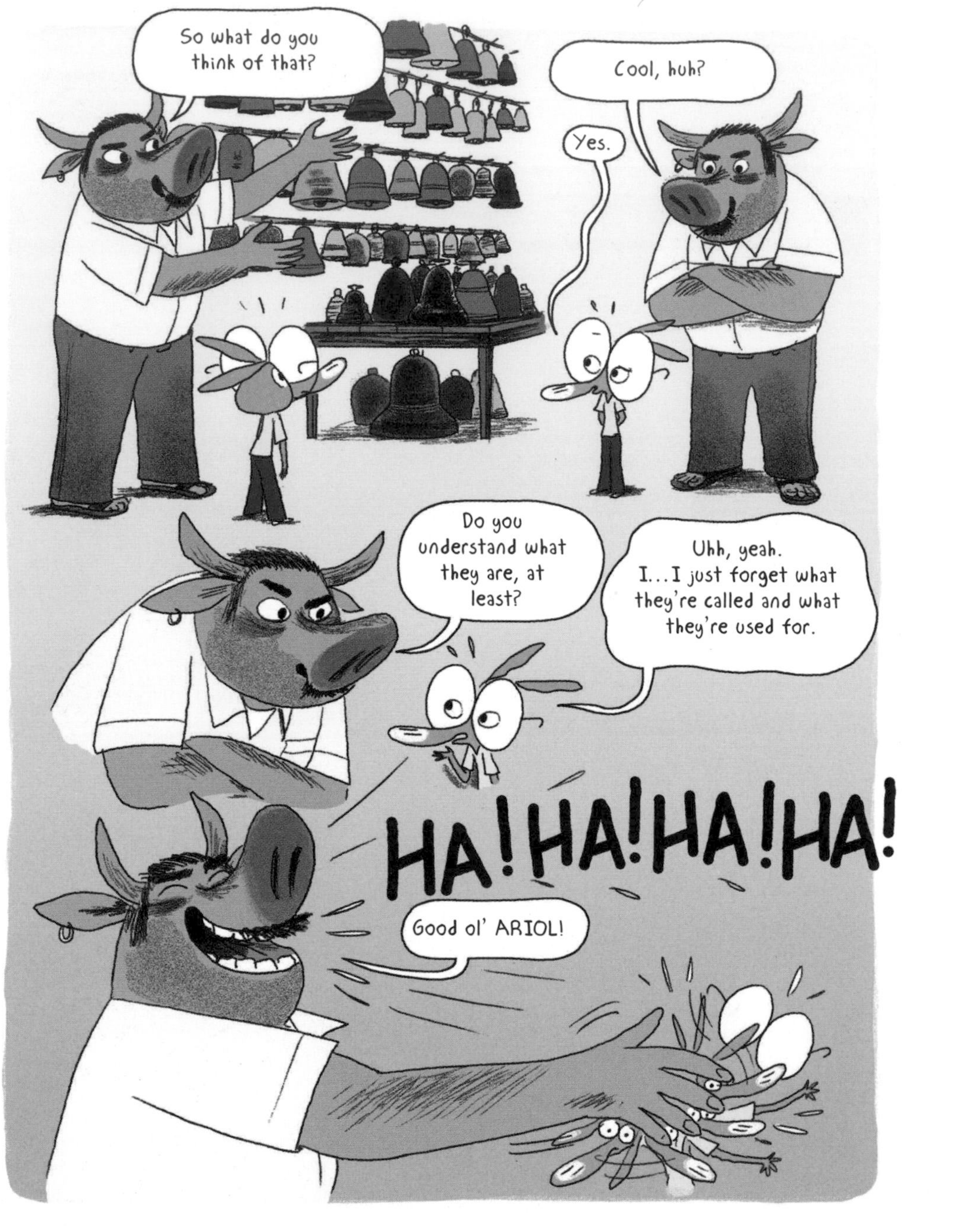
So what do you think of that?
Cool, huh?
Yes.
Do you understand what they are, at least?
Uhh, yeah. I...I just forget what they're called and what they're used for.
HA!HA!HA!HA!
Good ol' ARIOL!

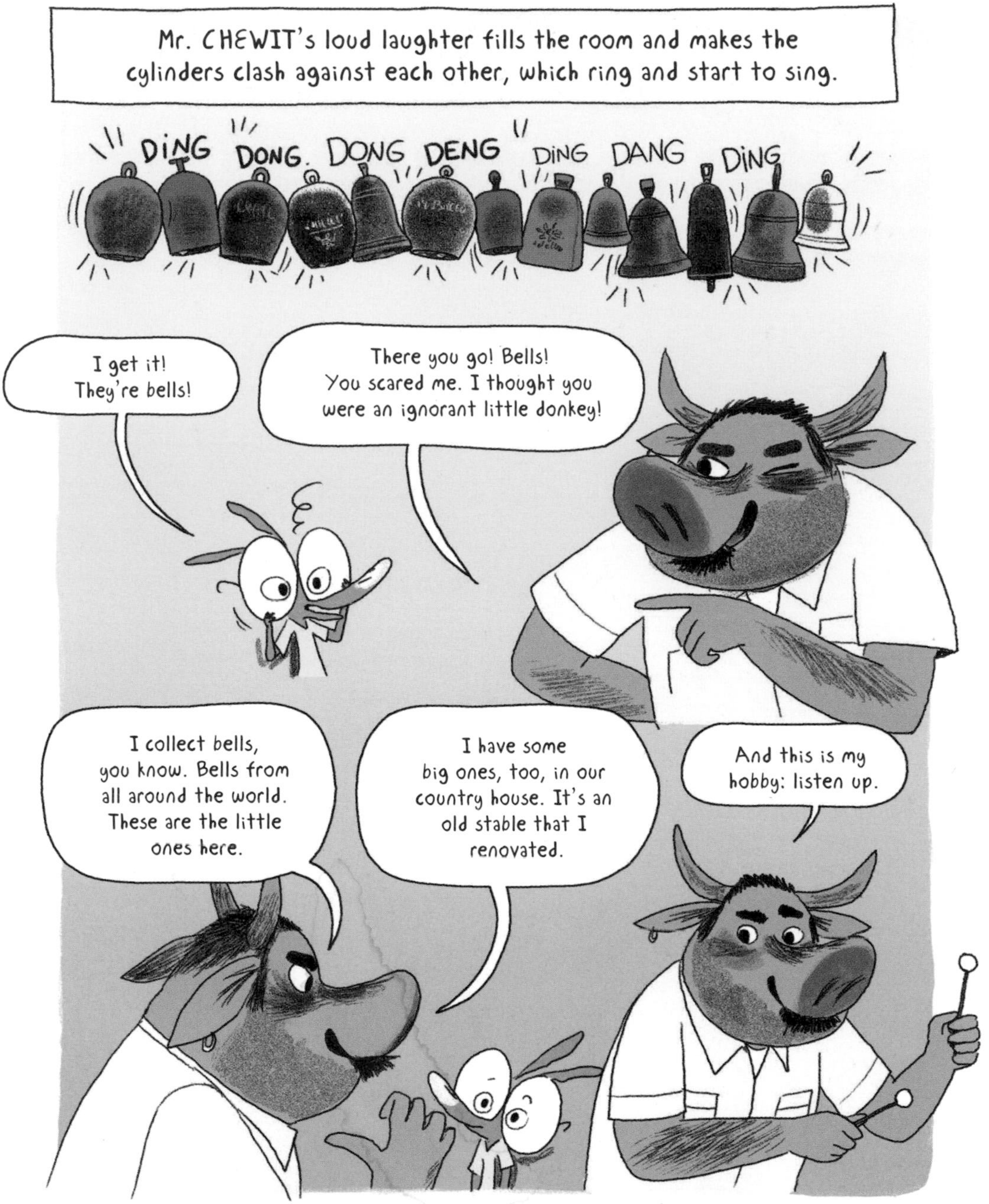
Mr. CHEWIT's loud laughter fills the room and makes the cylinders clash against each other, which ring and start to sing.
DING DONG. DONG DENG DING DANG DING
I get it! They're bells!
There you go! Bells! You scared me. I thought you were an ignorant little donkey!
I collect bells, you know. Bells from all around the world. These are the little ones here.
I have some big ones, too, in our country house. It's an old stable that I renovated.
And this is my hobby: listen up.

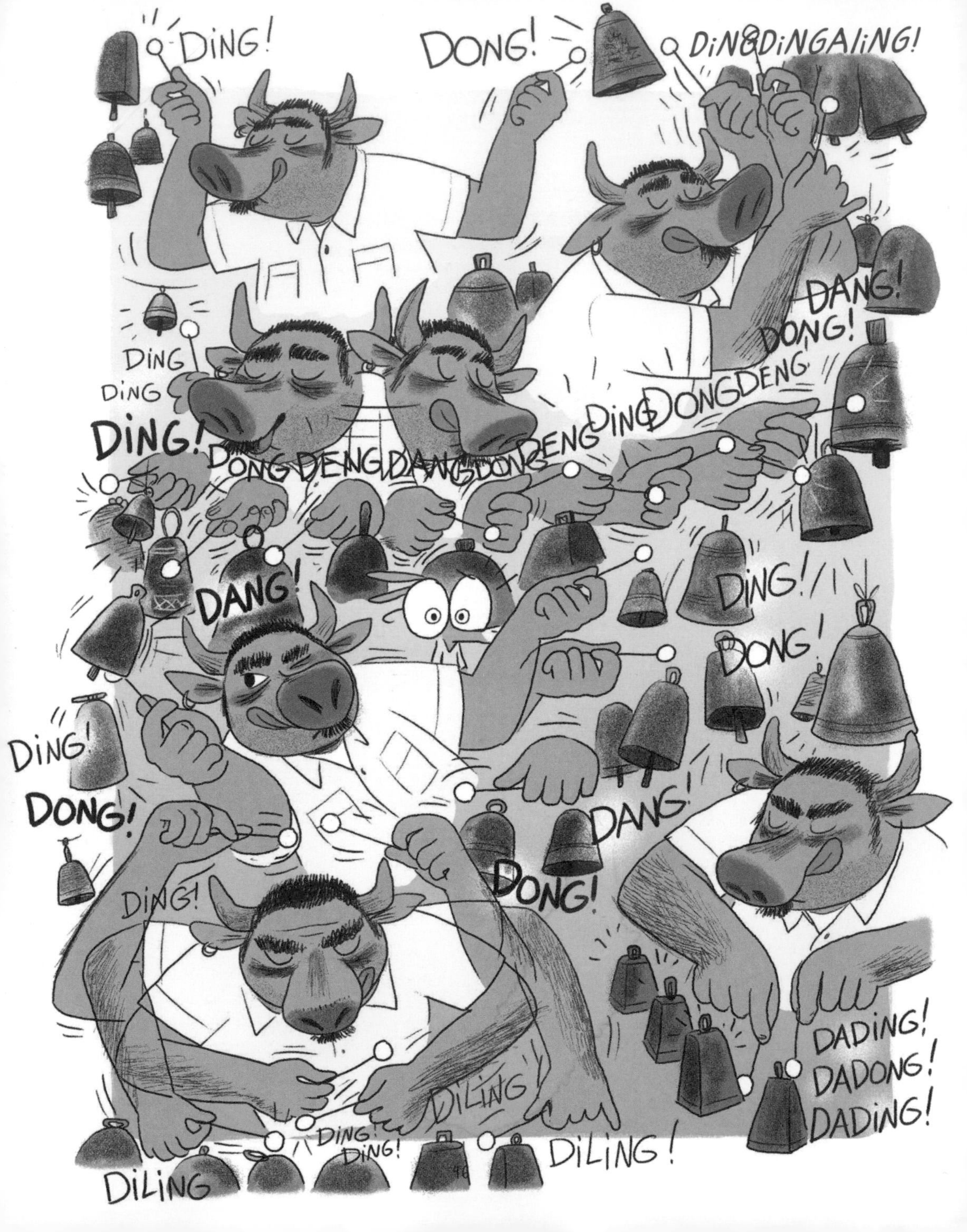
DING!
DONG!
DINGDINGALING!
DANG!
DONG!
DING
DING
DONGDENG
DING
DING!
DONG DENG DANG DONG DENG
DANG!
DING!
DONG!
DING!
DONG!
DANG!
DONG!
DING!
DADING!
DADONG!
DADING!
DILING
DING!
DING!
DILING!
DILING

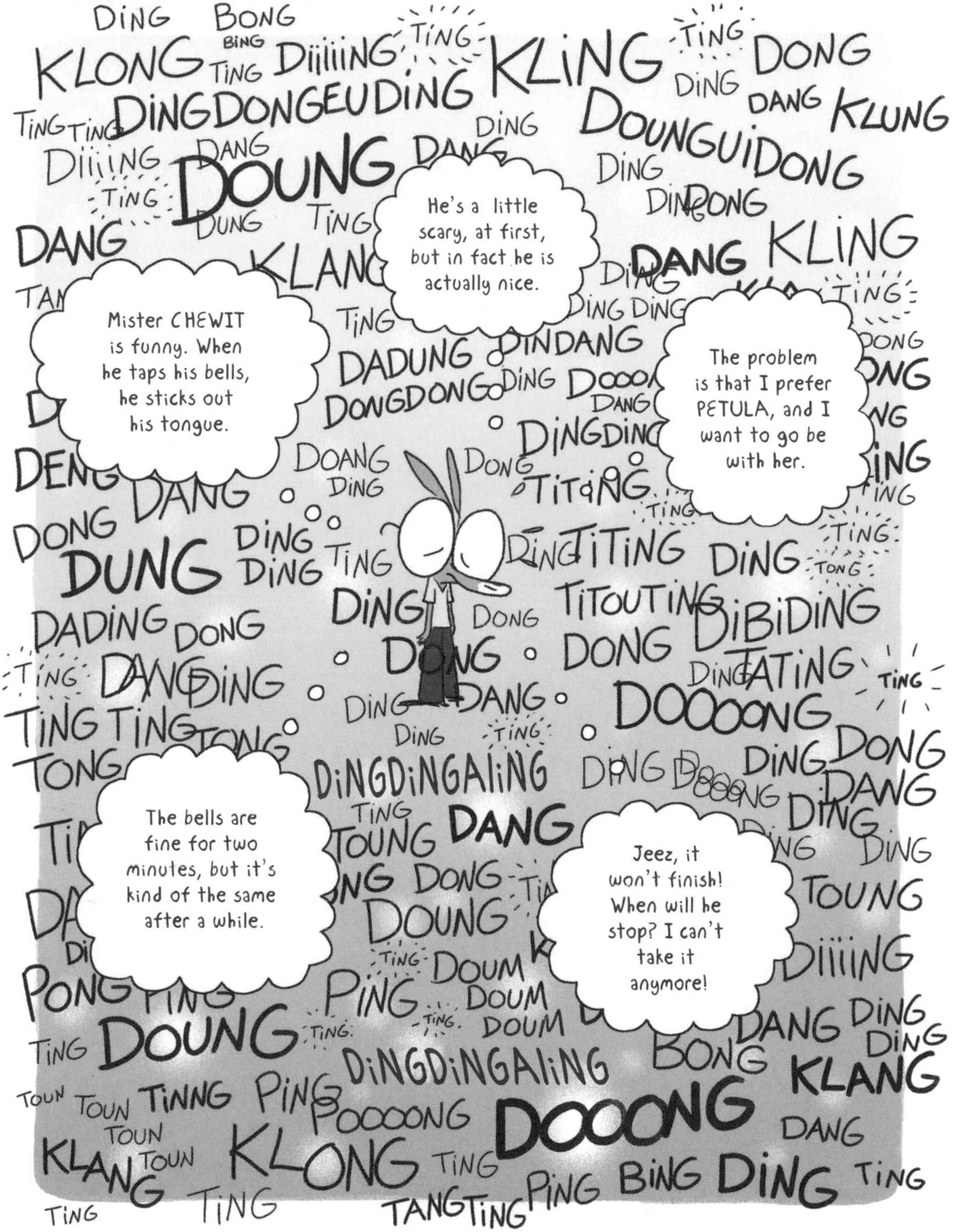
Mister CHEWIT is funny. When he taps his bells, he sticks out his tongue.
He's a little scary, at first, but in fact he is actually nice.
The problem is that I prefer PETULA, and I want to go be with her.
The bells are fine for two minutes, but it's kind of the same after a while.
Jeez, it won't finish! When will he stop? I can't take it anymore!

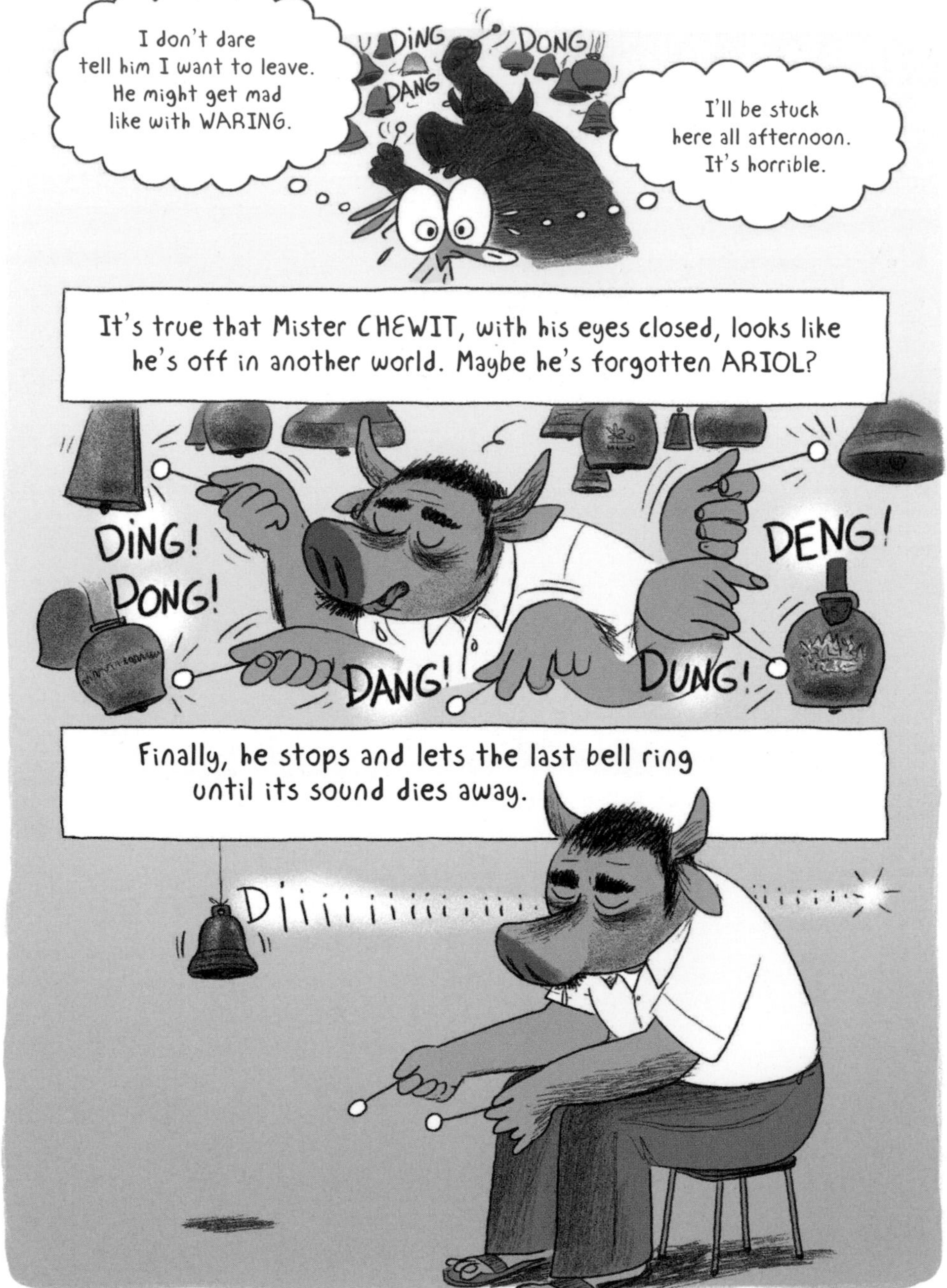
I don't dare tell him I want to leave. He might get mad like with WARING.
DING
DONG
DANG
I'll be stuck here all afternoon. It's horrible.
It's true that Mister CHEWIT, with his eyes closed, looks like he's off in another world. Maybe he's forgotten ARIOL?
DING!
DONG!
DANG!
DUNG!
DENG!
Finally, he stops and lets the last bell ring until its sound dies away.
Diiiiiiiiiiiii

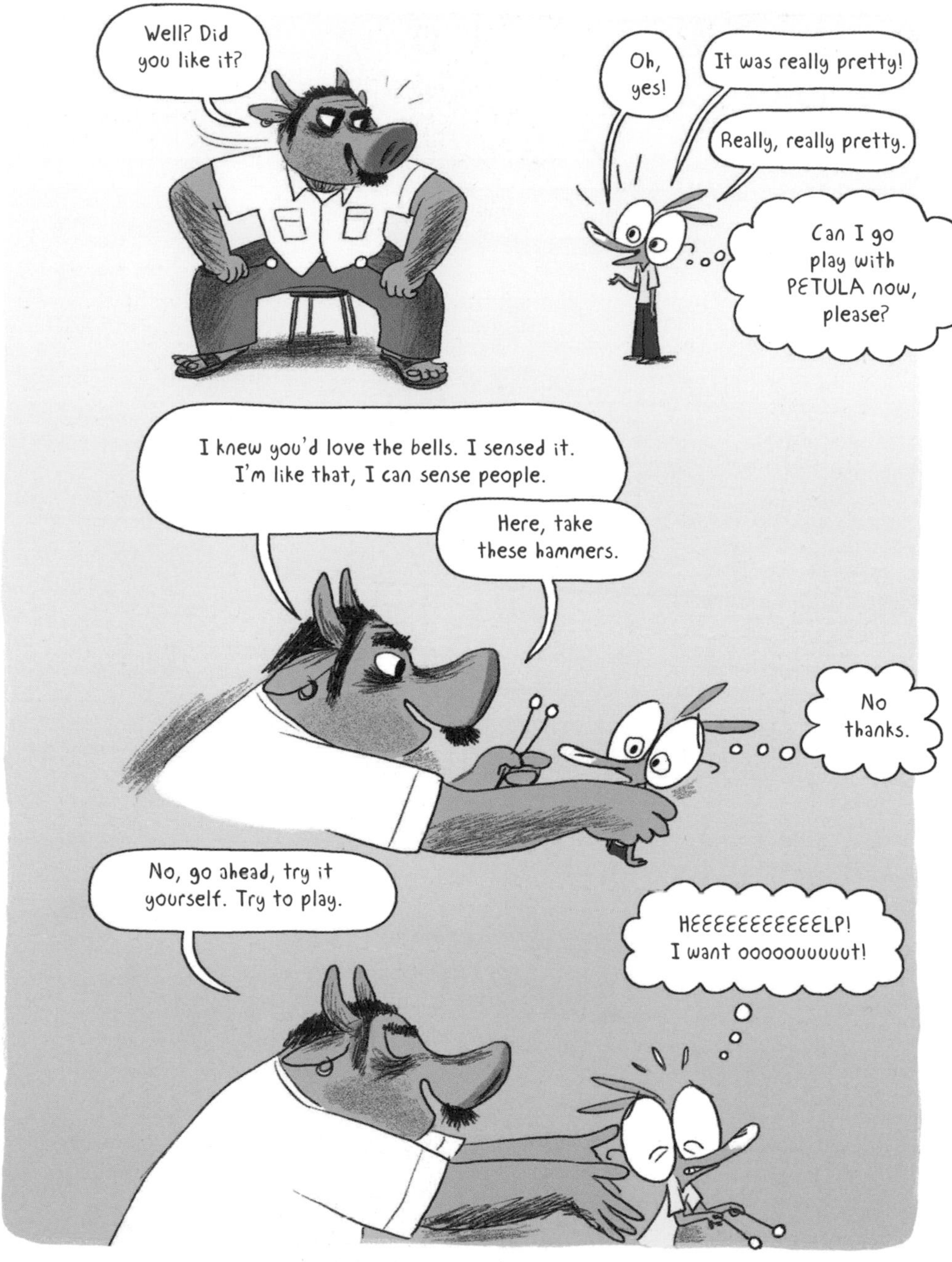
Well? Did you like it?
Oh, yes!
It was really pretty!
Really, really pretty.
Can I go play with PETULA now, please?
I knew you'd love the bells. I sensed it. I'm like that, I can sense people.
Here, take these hammers.
No thanks.
No, go ahead, try it yourself. Try to play.
HEEEEEEEEEEELP! I want oooouuuuut!

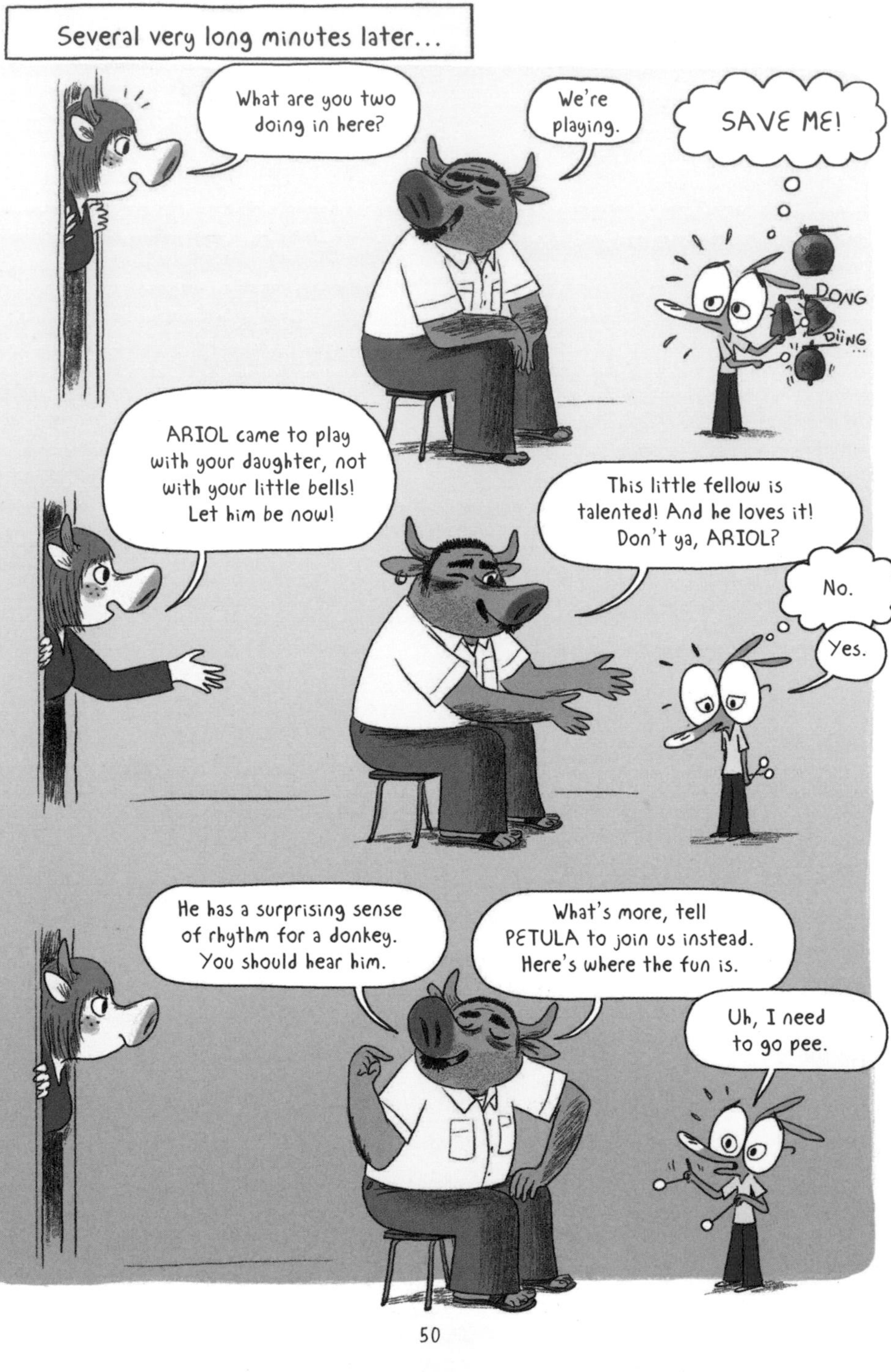
Several very long minutes later...
What are you two doing in here?
We're playing.
SAVE ME!
DONG
DIING...
ARIOL came to play with your daughter, not with your little bells! Let him be now!
This little fellow is talented! And he loves it! Don't ya, ARIOL?
No.
Yes.
He has a surprising sense of rhythm for a donkey. You should hear him.
What's more, tell PETULA to join us instead. Here's where the fun is.
Uh, I need to go pee.

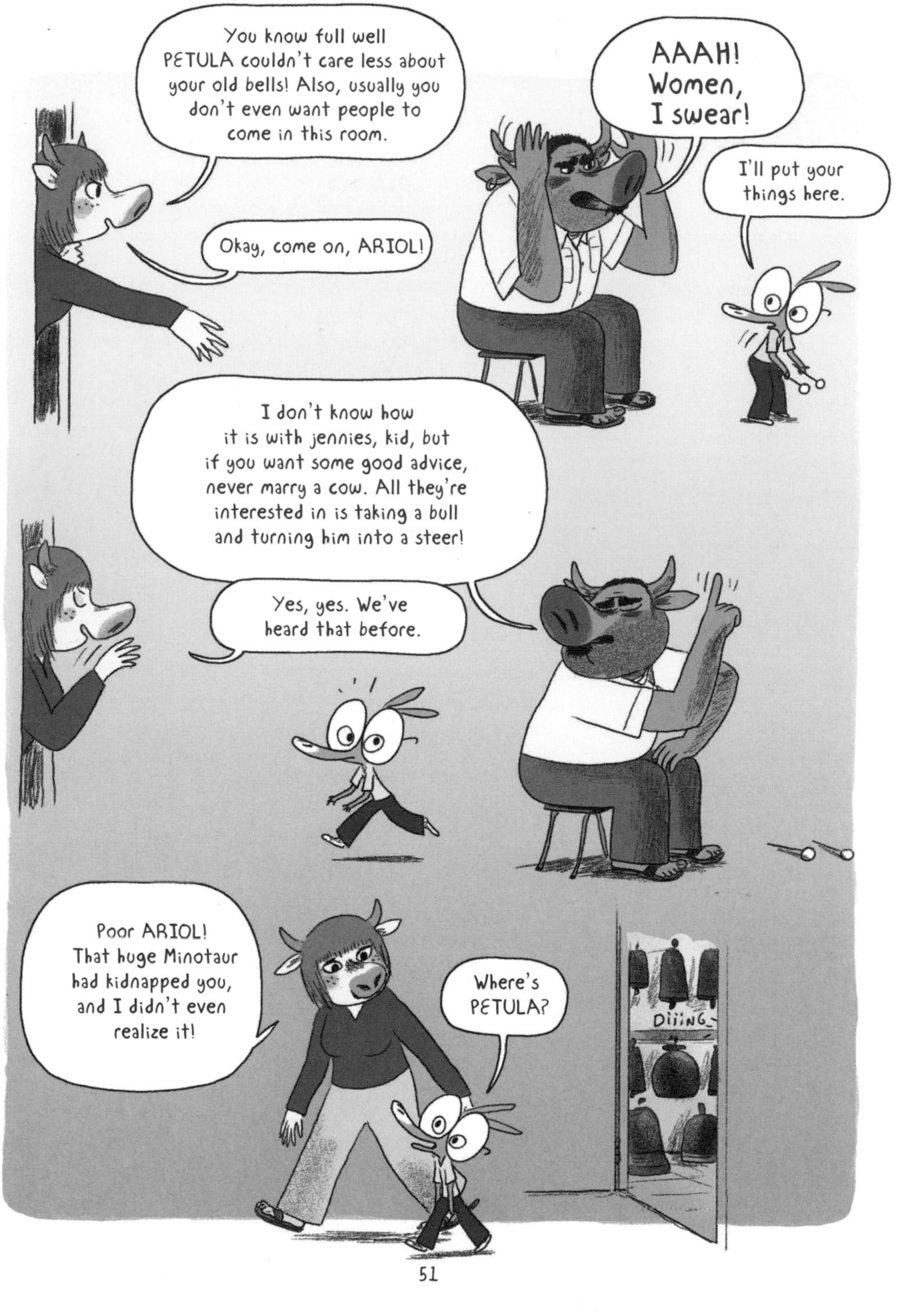
You know full well PETULA couldn't care less about your old bells! Also, usually you don't even want people to come in this room.
AAAH! Women, I swear!
I'll put your things here.
Okay, come on, ARIOL!
I don't know how it is with jennies, kid, but if you want some good advice, never marry a cow. All they're interested in is taking a bull and turning him into a steer!
Yes, yes. We've heard that before.
Poor ARIOL! That huge Minotaur had kidnapped you, and I didn't even realize it!
Where's PETULA?
DIIING_

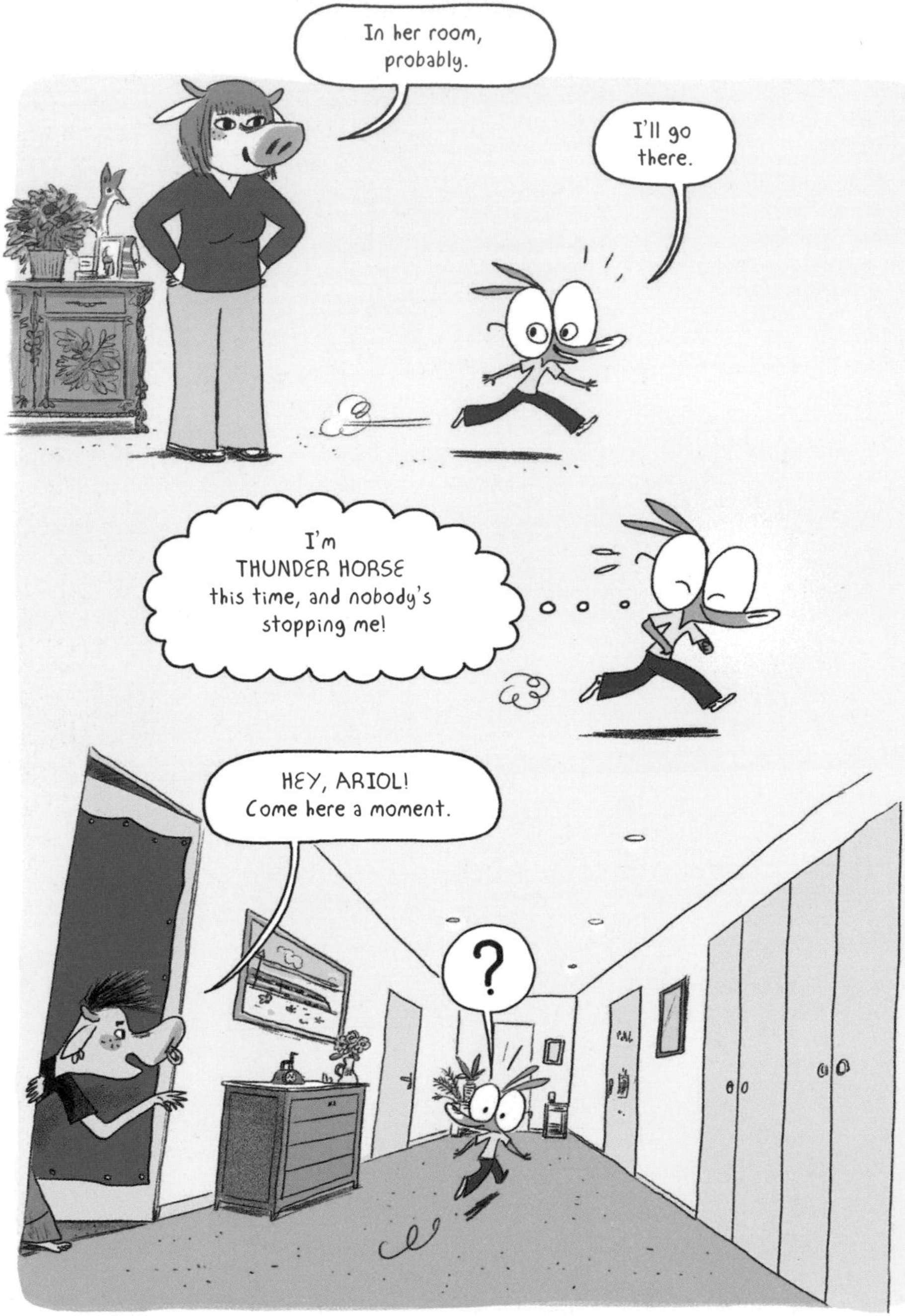
In her room, probably.
I'll go there.
I'm THUNDER HORSE this time, and nobody's stopping me!
HEY, ARIOL! Come here a moment.
?

CHAPTER 8

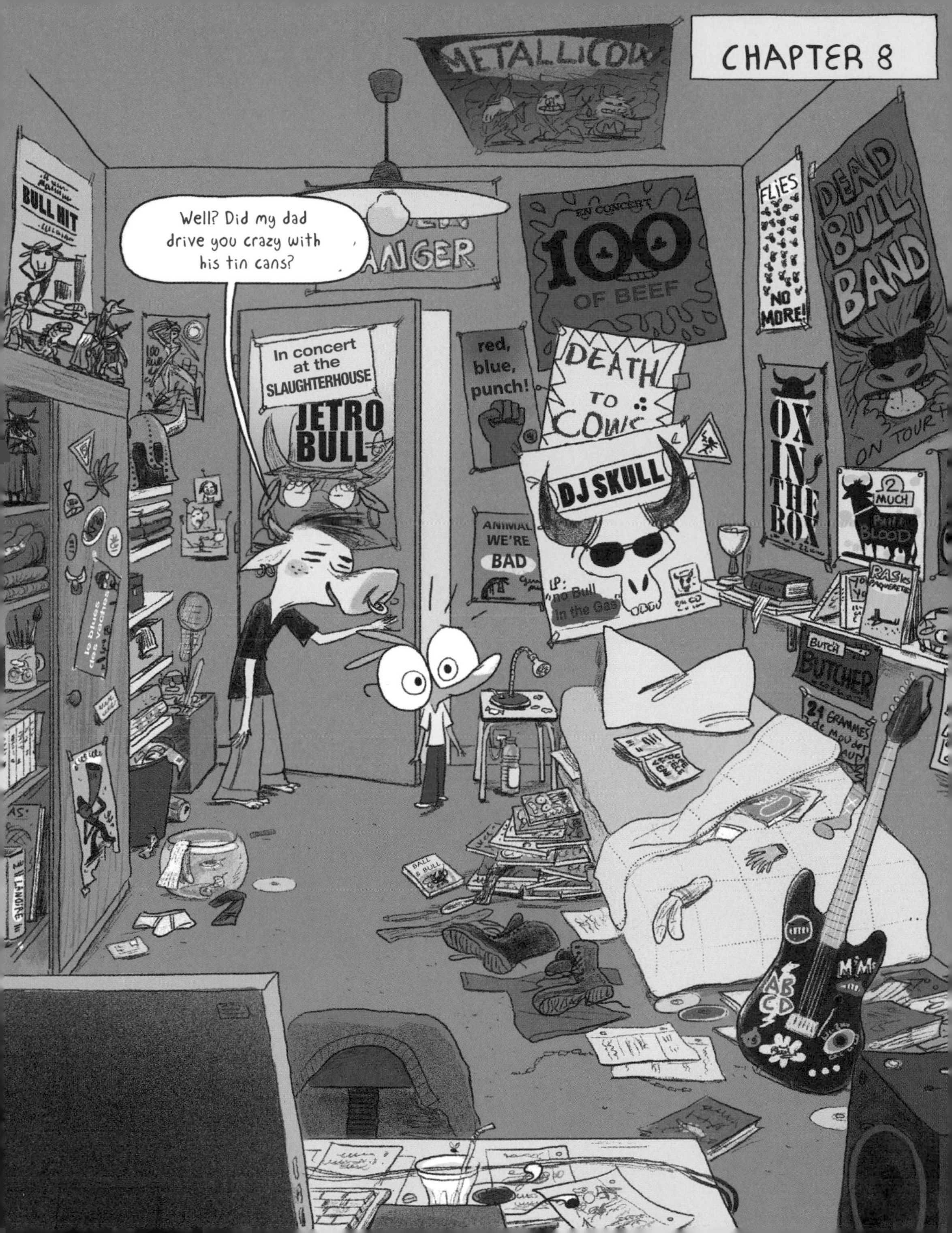
Well? Did my dad drive you crazy with his tin cans?
METALLICOW
BULL HIT
EN CONCERT
100
OF BEEF
FLIES
NO MORE!
DEAD BULL BAND
ON TOUR
In concert at the SLAUGHTERHOUSE
JETRO BULL
red, blue, punch!
DEATH TO
DJ SKULL
LP: "no Bull In the Gas
WE'RE BAD
OX IN THE BOX
2 MUCH
BLOOD
RAS les PAQUERETTES
BUTCH'S
BUTCHER
le blues des vaches
BALL & BULL

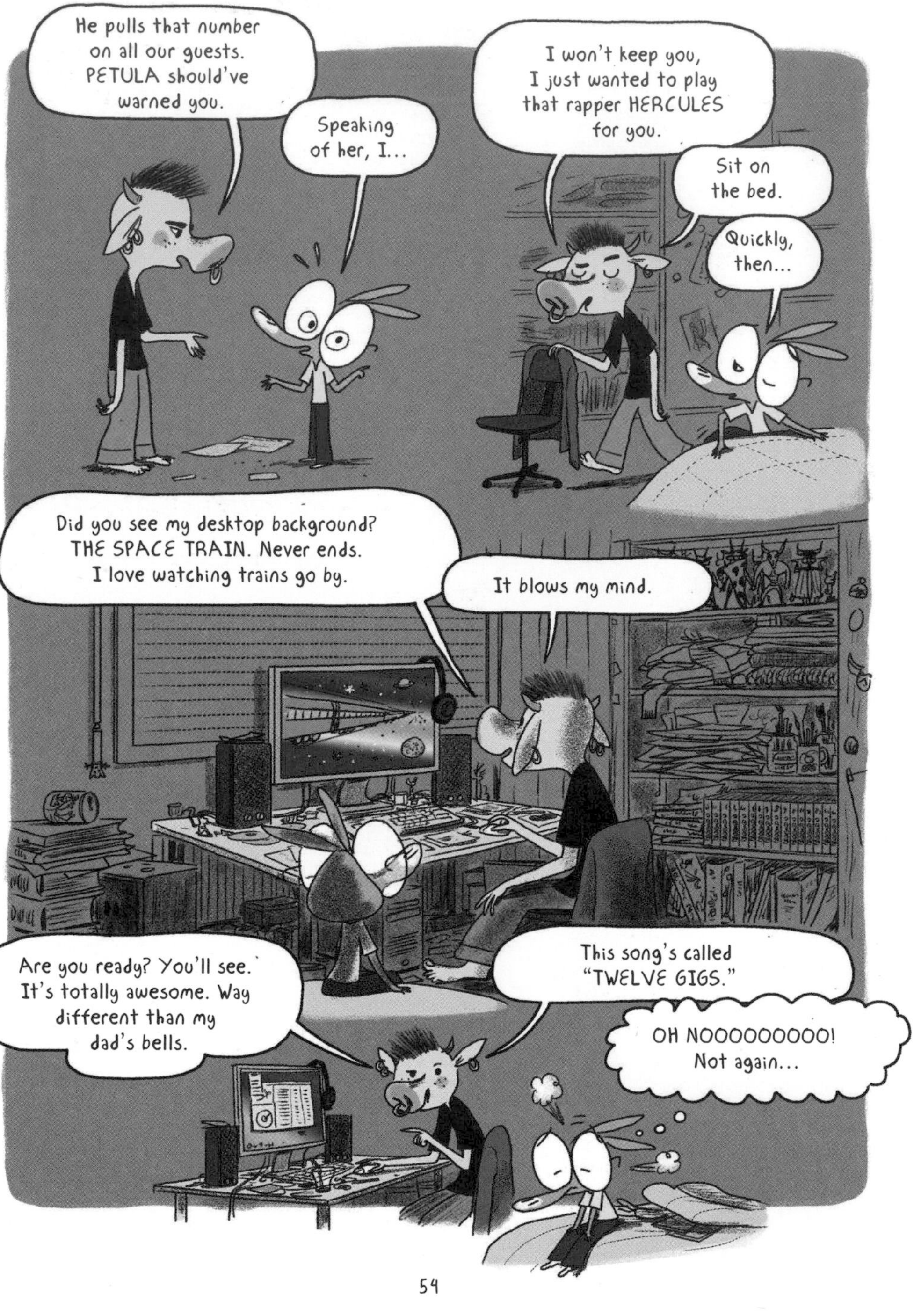
He pulls that number on all our guests. PETULA should've warned you.
Speaking of her, I...
I won't keep you, I just wanted to play that rapper HERCULES for you.
Sit on the bed.
Quickly, then...
Did you see my desktop background? THE SPACE TRAIN. Never ends. I love watching trains go by.
It blows my mind.
Are you ready? You'll see. It's totally awesome. Way different than my dad's bells.
This song's called "TWELVE GIGS."
OH NOOOOOOOOO! Not again...

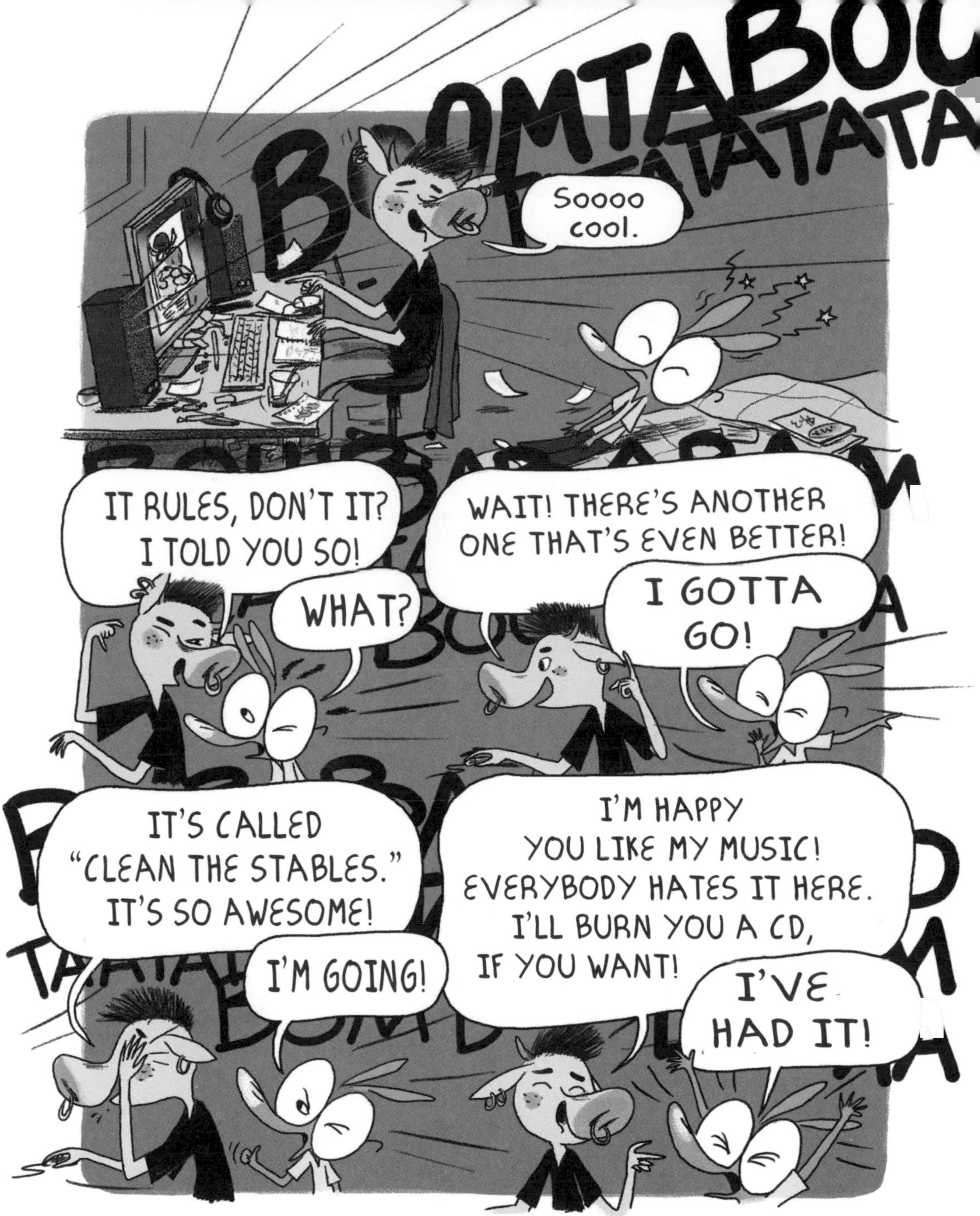
BOOMTABOU
TATATATA
Soooo cool.
IT RULES, DON'T IT? I TOLD YOU SO!
WHAT?
WAIT! THERE'S ANOTHER ONE THAT'S EVEN BETTER!
I GOTTA GO!
IT'S CALLED "CLEAN THE STABLES." IT'S SO AWESOME!
I'M GOING!
I'M HAPPY YOU LIKE MY MUSIC! EVERYBODY HATES IT HERE. I'LL BURN YOU A CD, IF YOU WANT!
I'VE HAD IT!

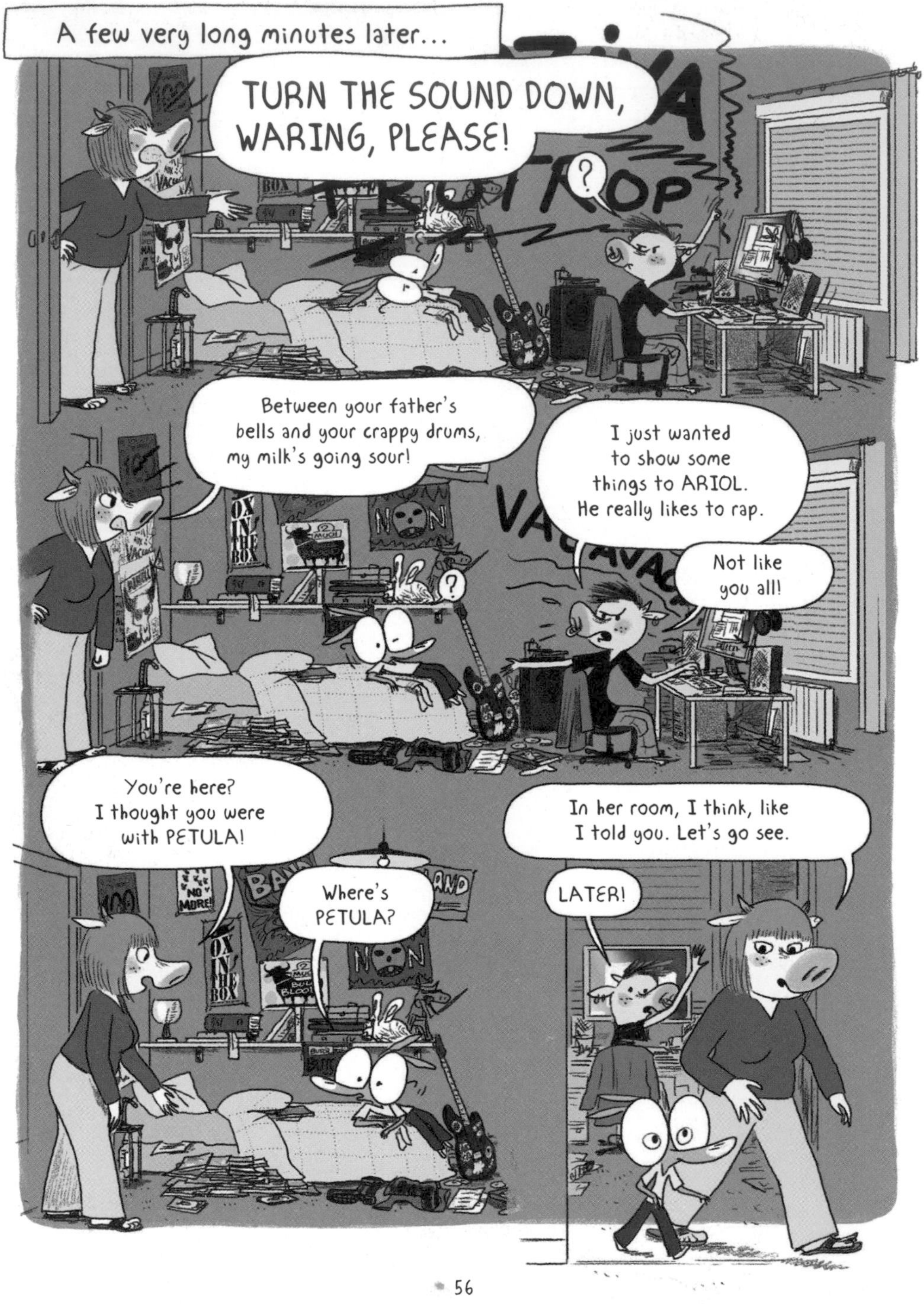

A few very long minutes later...
TURN THE SOUND DOWN, WARING, PLEASE!
?
Between your father's bells and your crappy drums, my milk's going sour!
I just wanted to show some things to ARIOL. He really likes to rap.
Not like you all!
?
You're here? I thought you were with PETULA!
Where's PETULA?
In her room, I think, like I told you. Let's go see.
LATER!

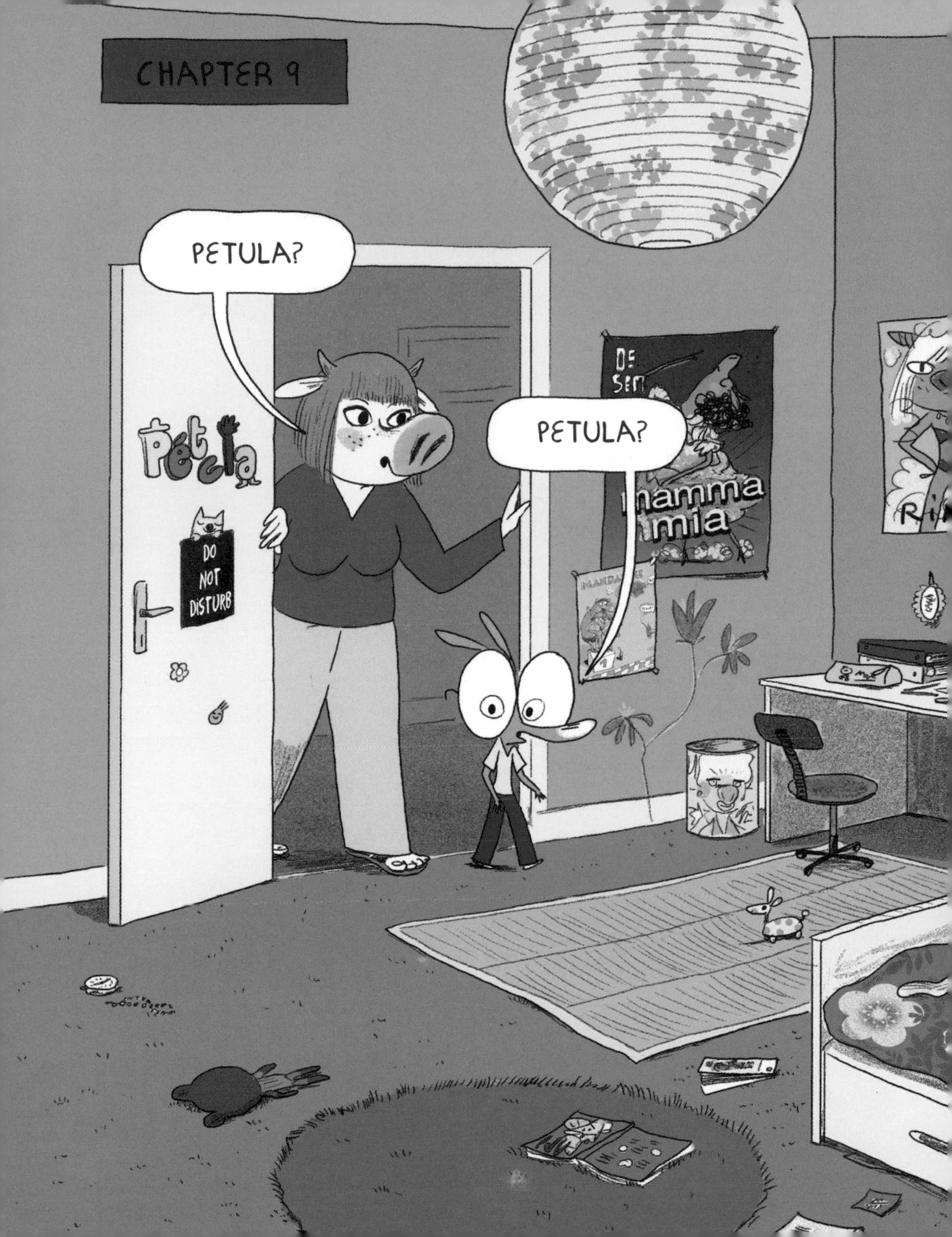
CHAPTER 9
PETULA?
PETULA?
DO NOT DISTURB
mamma mia

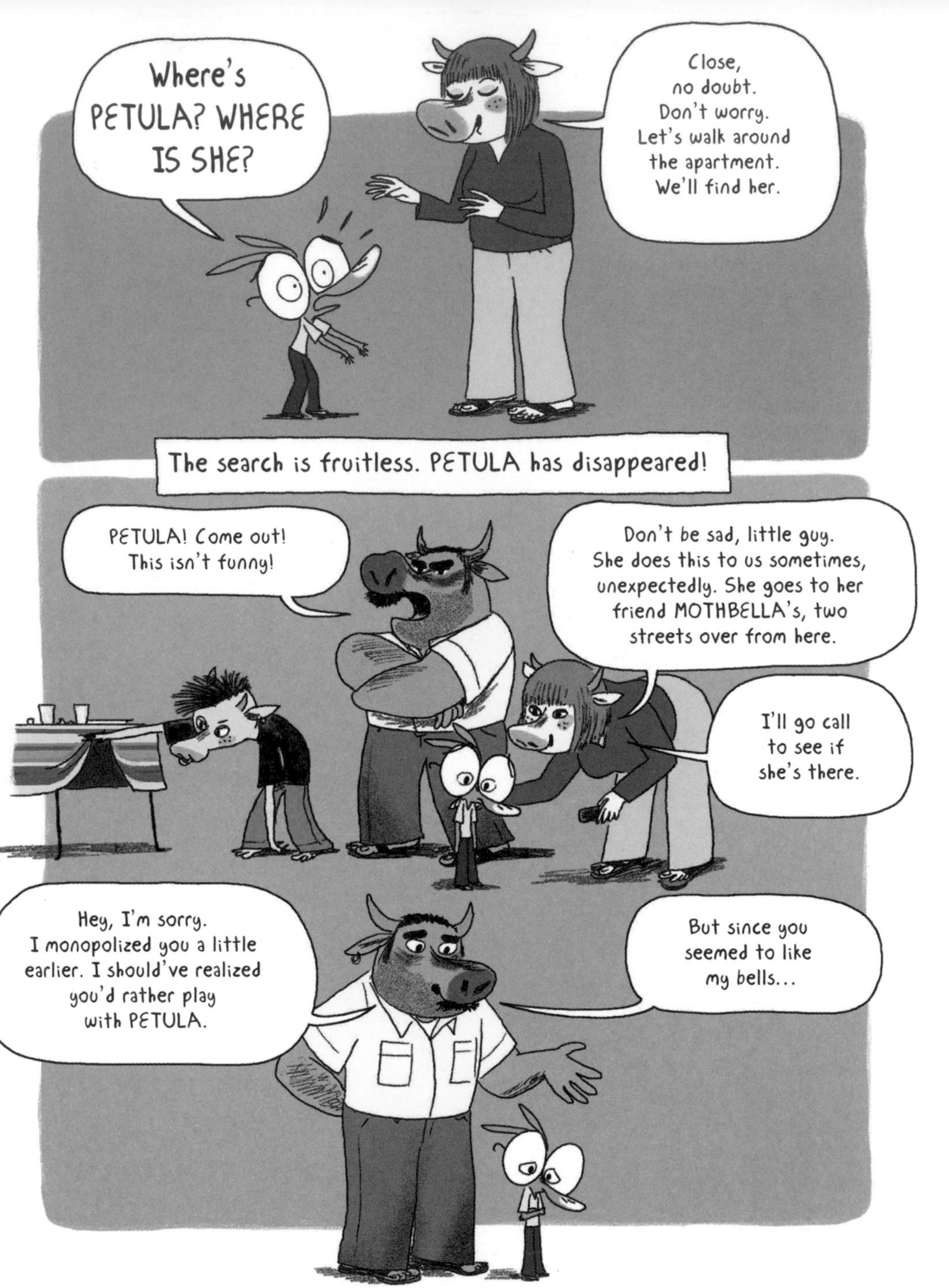
Where's PETULA? WHERE IS SHE?
Close, no doubt. Don't worry. Let's walk around the apartment. We'll find her.
The search is fruitless. PETULA has disappeared!
PETULA! Come out! This isn't funny!
Don't be sad, little guy. She does this to us sometimes, unexpectedly. She goes to her friend MOTHBELLA's, two streets over from here.
I'll go call to see if she's there.
Hey, I'm sorry. I monopolized you a little earlier. I should've realized you'd rather play with PETULA.
But since you seemed to like my bells...

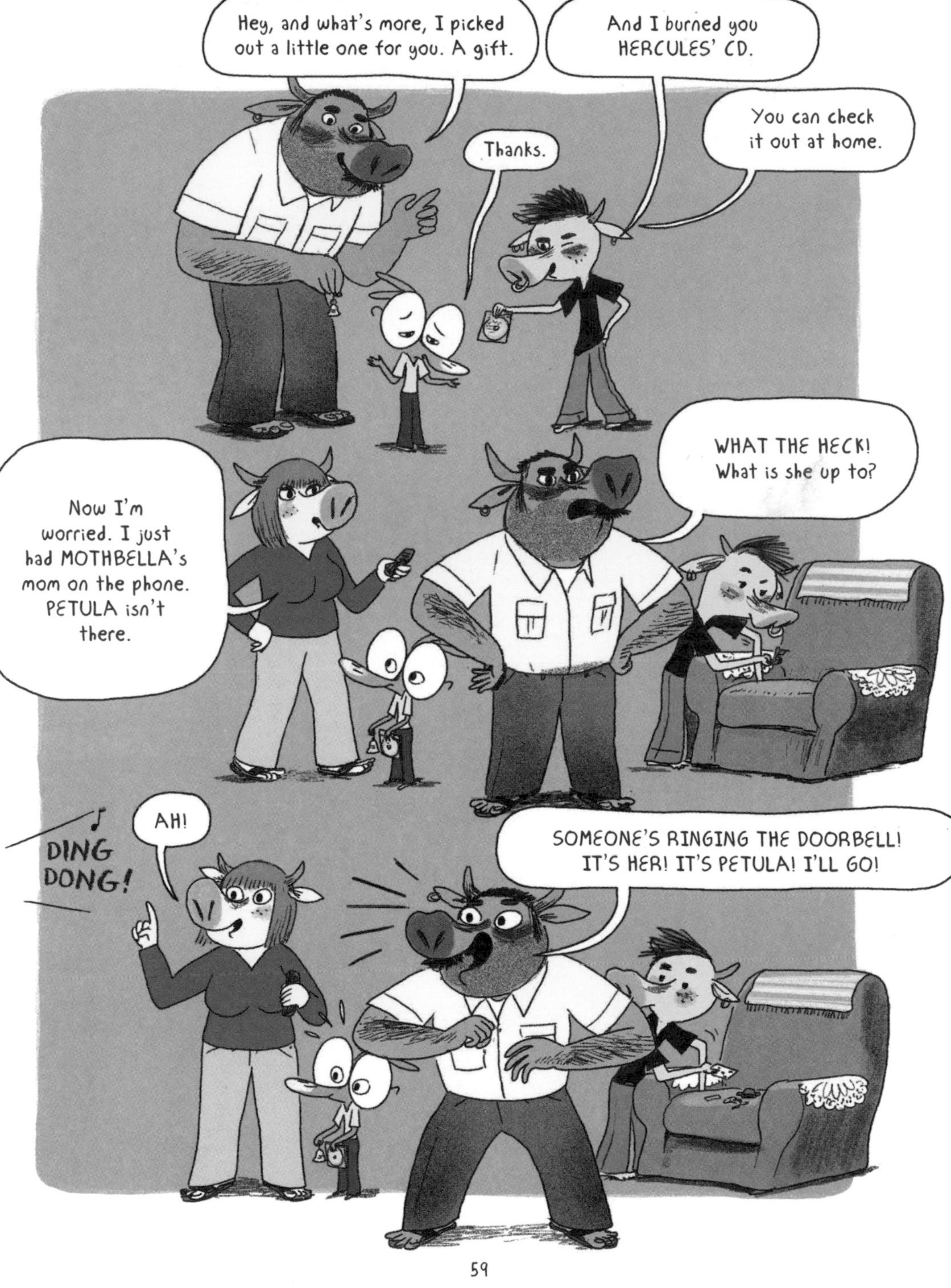
Hey, and what's more, I picked out a little one for you. A gift.
Thanks.
And I burned you HERCULES' CD.
You can check it out at home.
Now I'm worried. I just had MOTHBELLA's mom on the phone. PETULA isn't there.
WHAT THE HECK! What is she up to?
DING DONG!
AH!
SOMEONE'S RINGING THE DOORBELL! IT'S HER! IT'S PETULA! I'LL GO!

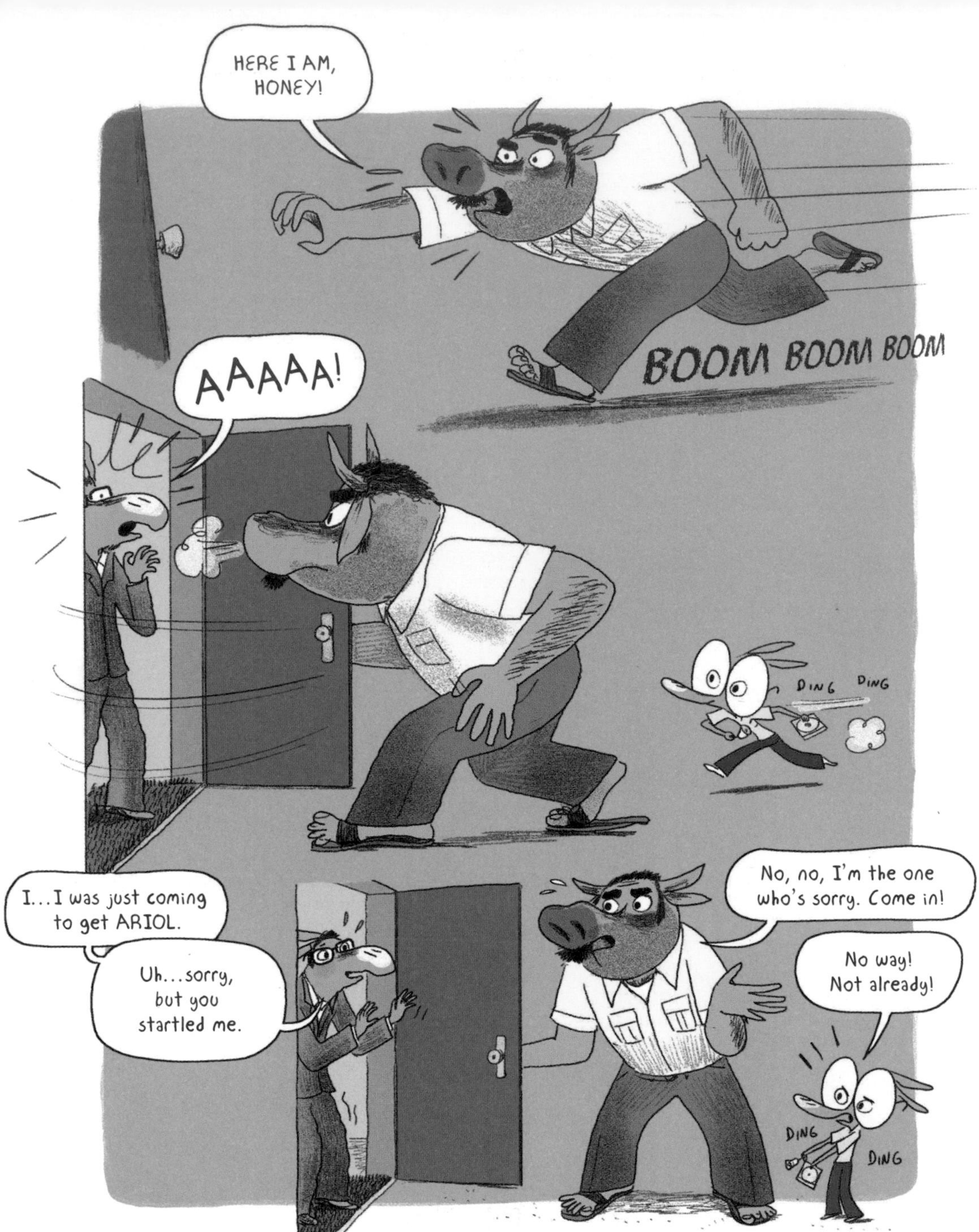
HERE I AM, HONEY!
BOOM BOOM BOOM
AAAAA!
DING DING
I...I was just coming to get ARIOL.
Uh...sorry, but you startled me.
No, no, I'm the one who's sorry. Come in!
No way! Not already!
DING DING

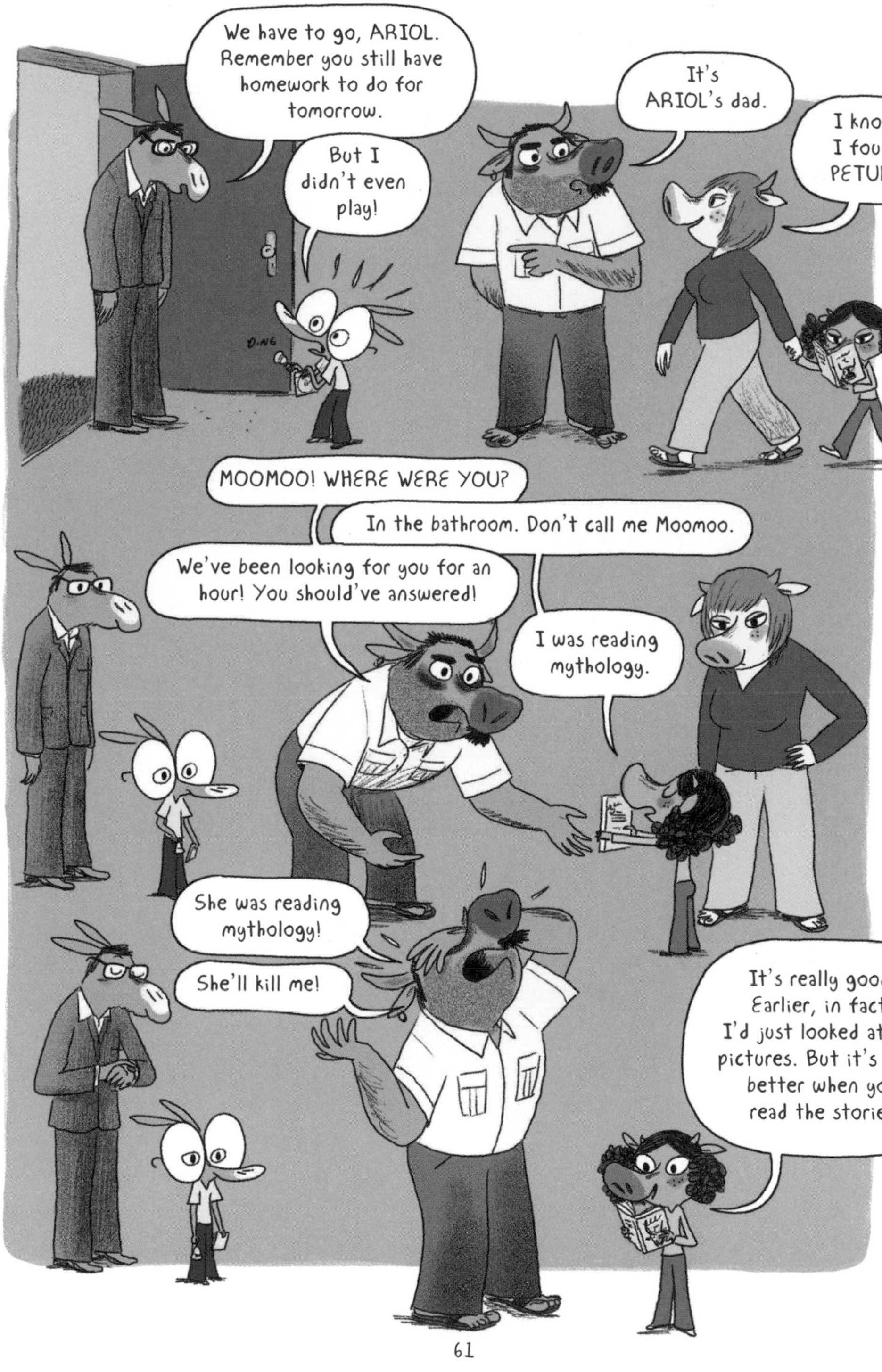
We have to go, ARIOL. Remember you still have homework to do for tomorrow.
But I didn't even play!
DING
It's ARIOL's dad.
I know. I found PETULA.
MOOMOO! WHERE WERE YOU?
In the bathroom. Don't call me Moomoo.
We've been looking for you for an hour! You should've answered!
I was reading mythology.
She was reading mythology!
She'll kill me!
It's really good. Earlier, in fact, I'd just looked at the pictures. But it's even better when you read the stories.

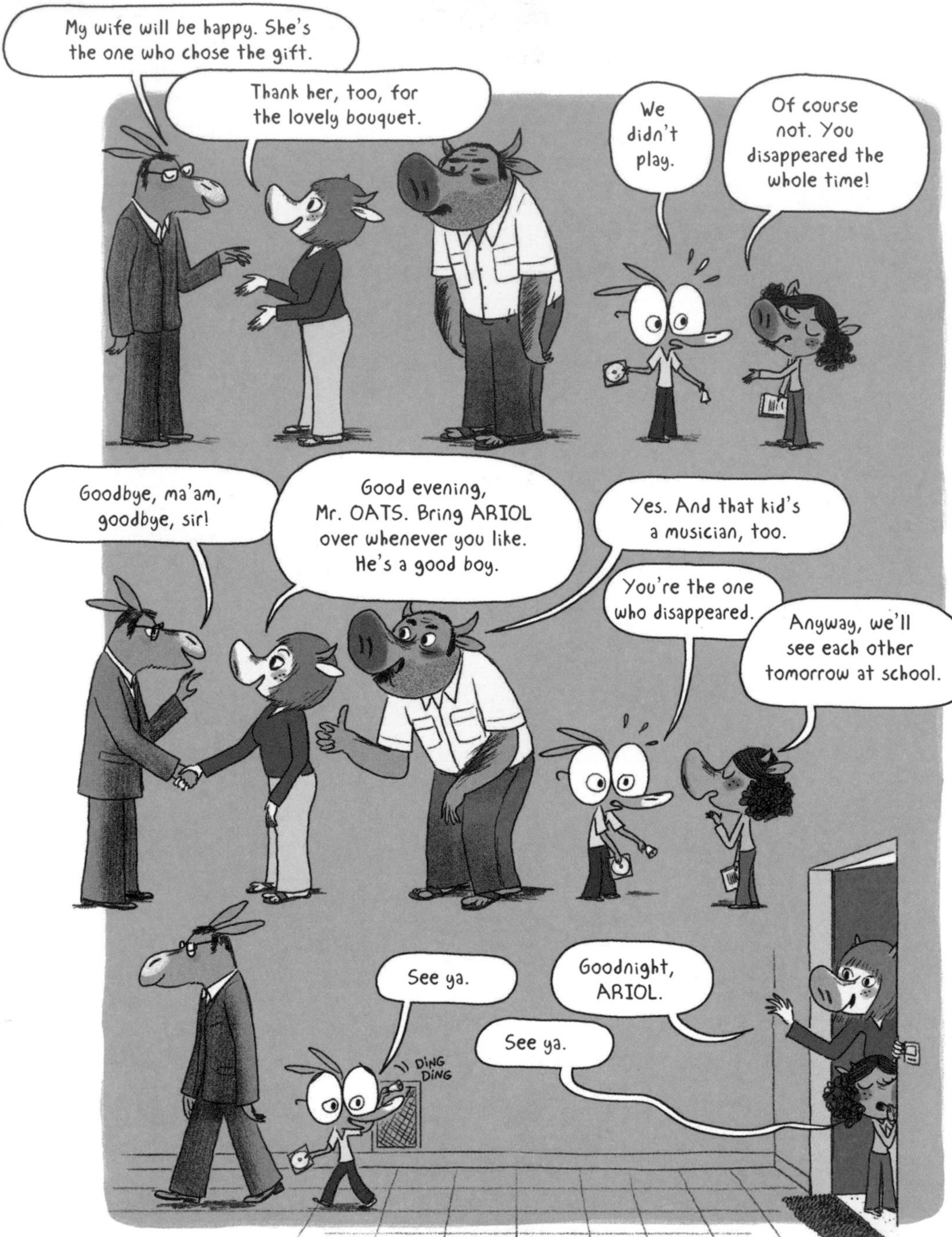

My wife will be happy. She's the one who chose the gift.
Thank her, too, for the lovely bouquet.
We didn't play.
Of course not. You disappeared the whole time!
Goodbye, ma'am, goodbye, sir!
Good evening, Mr. OATS. Bring ARIOL over whenever you like. He's a good boy.
Yes. And that kid's a musician, too.
You're the one who disappeared.
Anyway, we'll see each other tomorrow at school.
See ya.
DING DING
Goodnight, ARIOL.
See ya.

CHAPTER 10

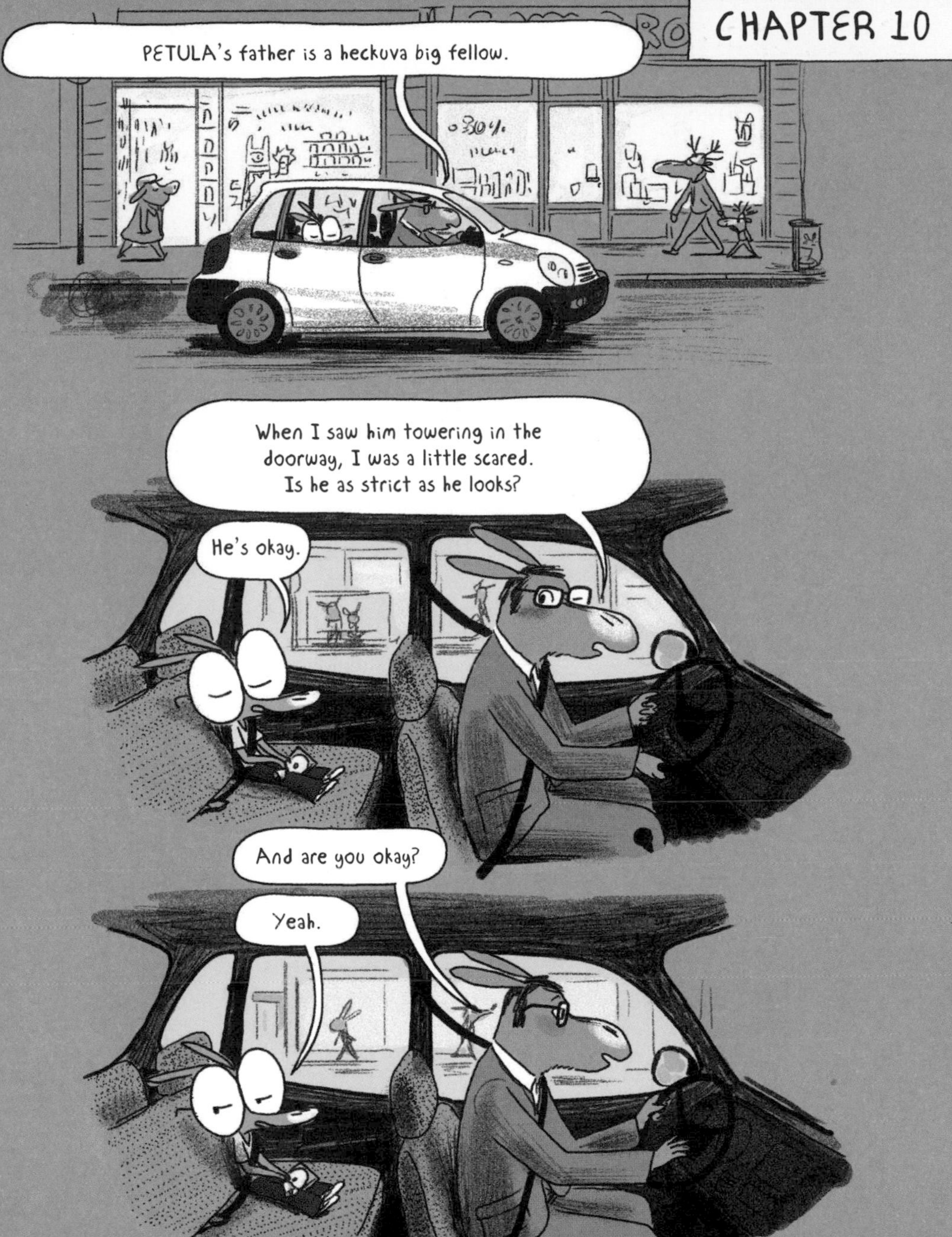

PETULA's father is a heckuva big fellow.
When I saw him towering in the doorway, I was a little scared. Is he as strict as he looks?
He's okay.
And are you okay?
Yeah.

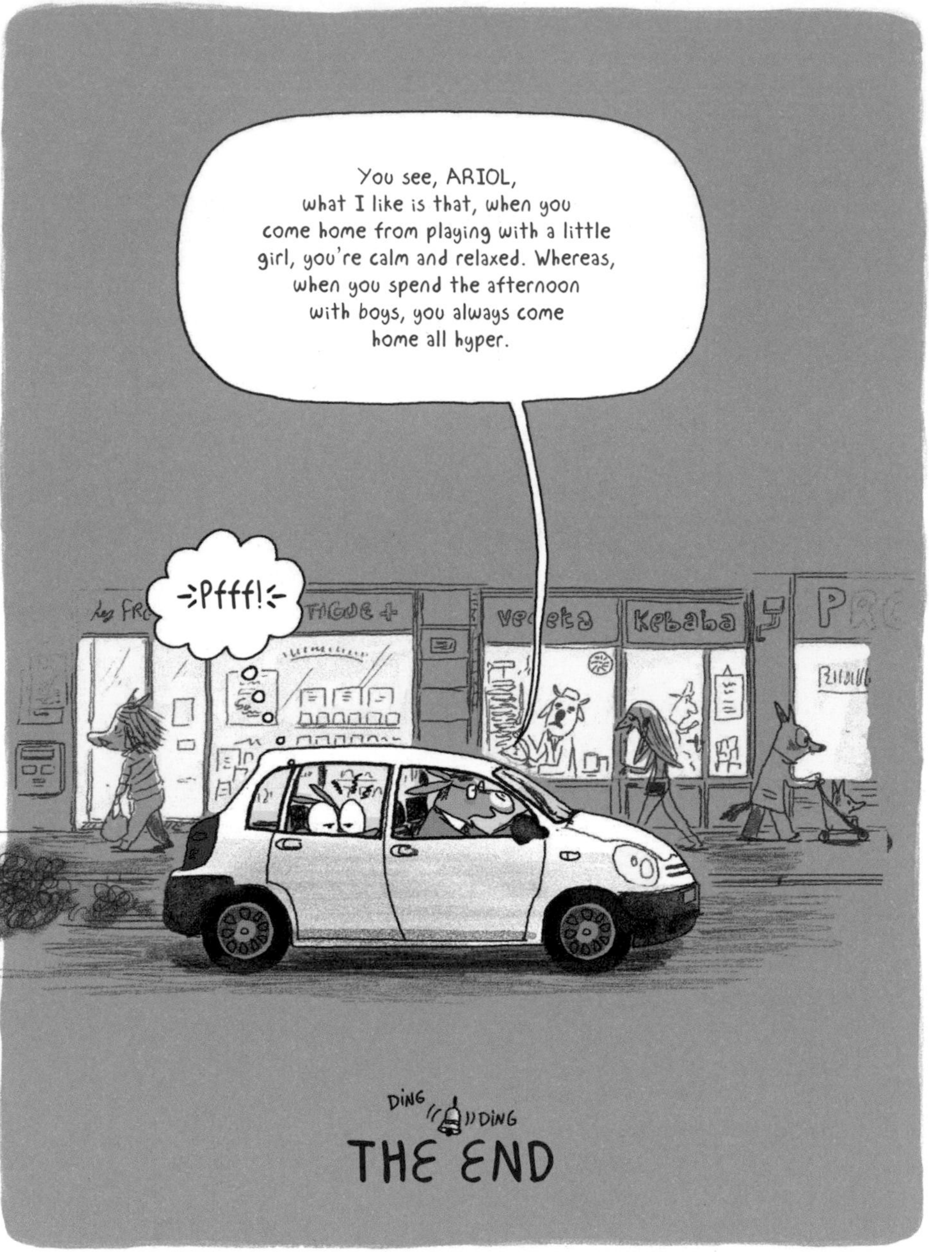
You see, ARIOL, what I like is that, when you come home from playing with a little girl, you're calm and relaxed. Whereas, when you spend the afternoon with boys, you always come home all hyper.
Pfff!
Vedetta
Kebaba
DING DING
THE END

WATCH OUT FOR PAPERCUTZ™

Welcome to the biggest single story starring Ariol yet, by Emmanuel Guibert and Marc Boutavant, from Papercutz, those humans with human heads dedicated to publishing great graphic novels for all ages. I'm Jim Salicrup, the Editor-in-Chief and Ariol's Life Coach.

If this is the very first time you've picked up an ARIOL graphic novel—CONGRATULATIONS! As you've no doubt noticed by now ARIOL is brilliantly written and beautifully drawn by Emmanuel and Marc. But the good news is, there are six other ARIOL graphic novels that you've yet to experience! Check out page 2 for the complete list. And don't forget that ARIOL graphic novels are also available digitally wherever e-books are sold. If you're like us, you probably can't get enough of ARIOL!

Normally, in our regularly published ARIOL graphic novel series, Ariol appears in a series of ten-page stories, but this graphic novel is special. Ariol winds up with a play date at the home of his secret true love, Petula. A story this important, this meaningful, this stupendous... demands to be told in more than a mere ten pages! After all, the story of Ariol simply walking Petula home (See in ARIOL #3 "Happy as a Pig...") took ten pages! Surely, the story of what happens inside Petula's home would have to be even longer. After all, this is the story of Ariol finally getting invited to the home of his true love. When one thinks of all the world's great romances—Romeo and Juliet, Liz and Dick, Homer and Marge, Kim and Kanye—it's possible folks may one day be thinking of Ariol and Petula as well! Or not. To keep an eye on this ever-developing romance, may I suggest that you don't miss ARIOL #7 "Top Dog." Who knows what may or may not happen next?!

Thanks,

Jim

STAY IN TOUCH!

EMAIL: salicrup@papercutz.com
WEB: papercutz.com
TWITTER: @papercutzgn
FACEBOOK: PAPERCUTZGRAPHICNOVELS
REGULAR MAIL: Papercutz, 160 Broadway,
Suite 700, East Wing,
New York, NY 10038

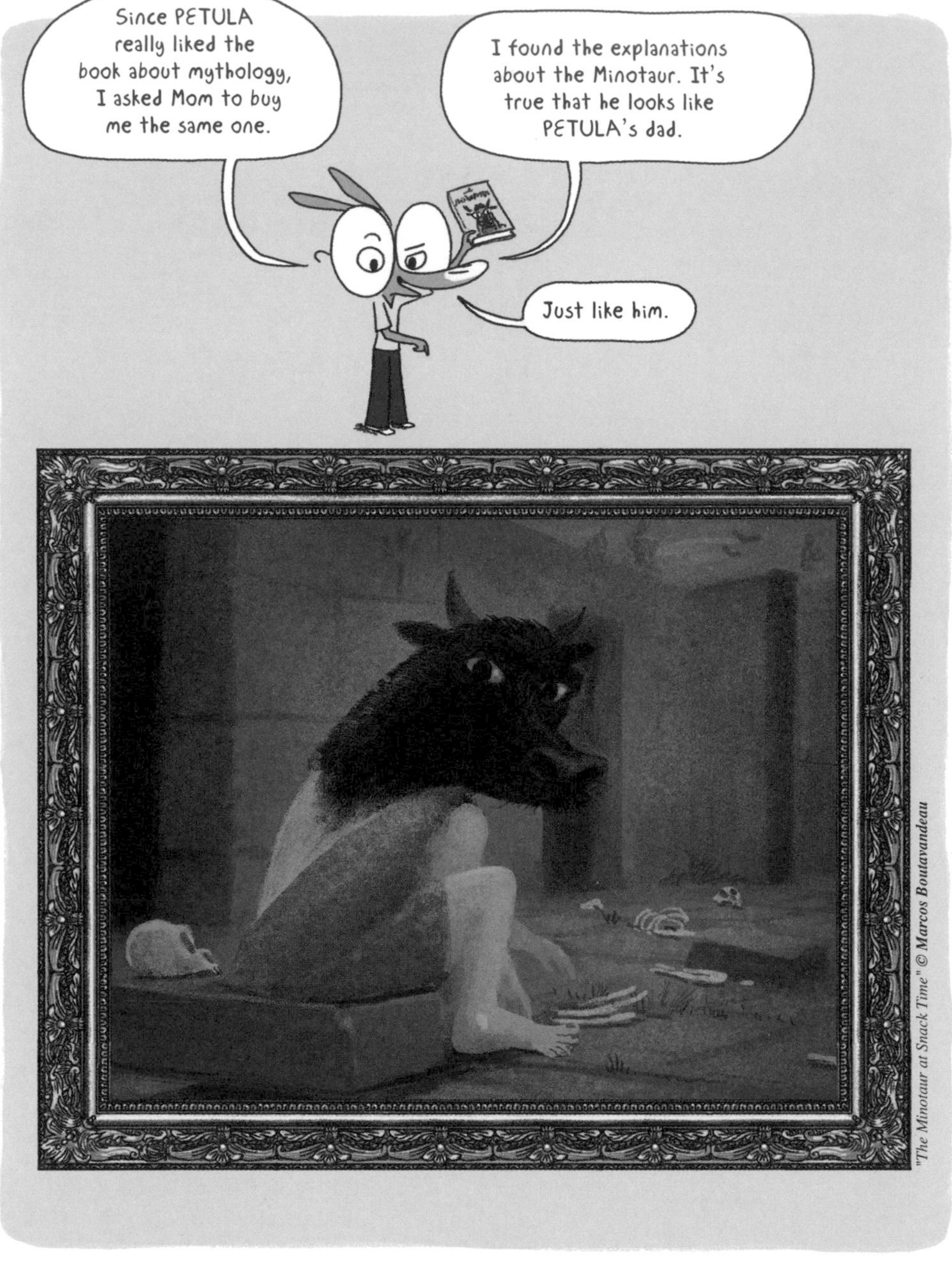
Since PETULA really liked the book about mythology, I asked Mom to buy me the same one.
I found the explanations about the Minotaur. It's true that he looks like PETULA's dad.
Just like him.
"The Minotaur at Snack Time" **© Marcos Boutavandeau**

THE MINOTAUR

Greek mythology tells the frightening story of the Minotaur, a monster with the head of a bull. The king of Crete, Minos, locked him inside an immense labyrinth in the center of his island. Regularly, young boys and girls were offered as sacrifices to the Minotaur.

Theseus, an Athenian, slipped in with the sacrifices one day to fight the Minotaur. He killed it and was able to get back out of the maze thanks to a ball of string he'd unwound along his path. This ball had been given to him by Ariadne, Minos' daughter, who was in love with Theseus.

People, today, still speak of ARIADNE'S THREAD to designate a precious asset that can get us out of a difficult situation. In French, a labyrinth is also called a "DÉDALE," after DAEDALUS, the architect of MINOS' labyrinth.

Whenever I read a book PETULA has read, it's kind of like I was with her.

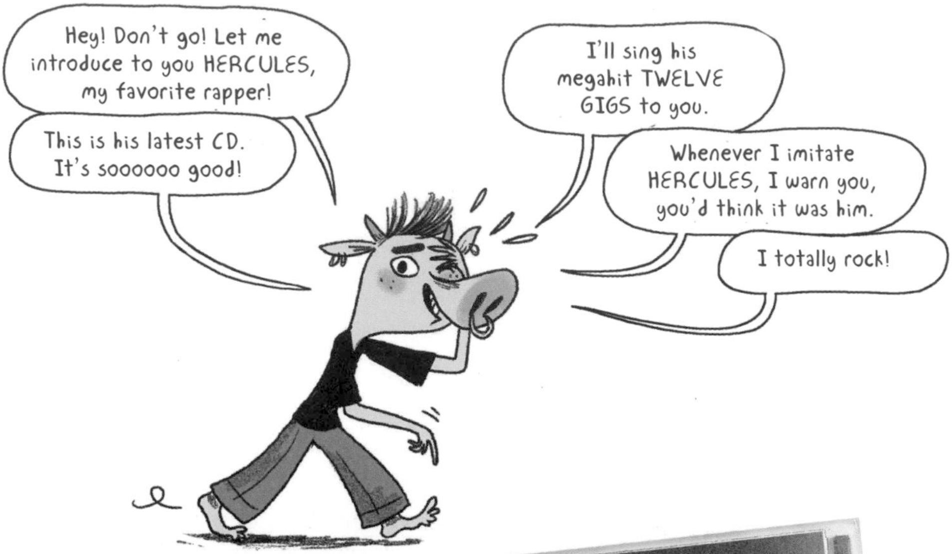
Hey! Don't go! Let me introduce to you HERCULES, my favorite rapper!
This is his latest CD. It's soooooo good!
I'll sing his megahit TWELVE GIGS to you.
Whenever I imitate HERCULES, I warn you, you'd think it was him.
I totally rock!

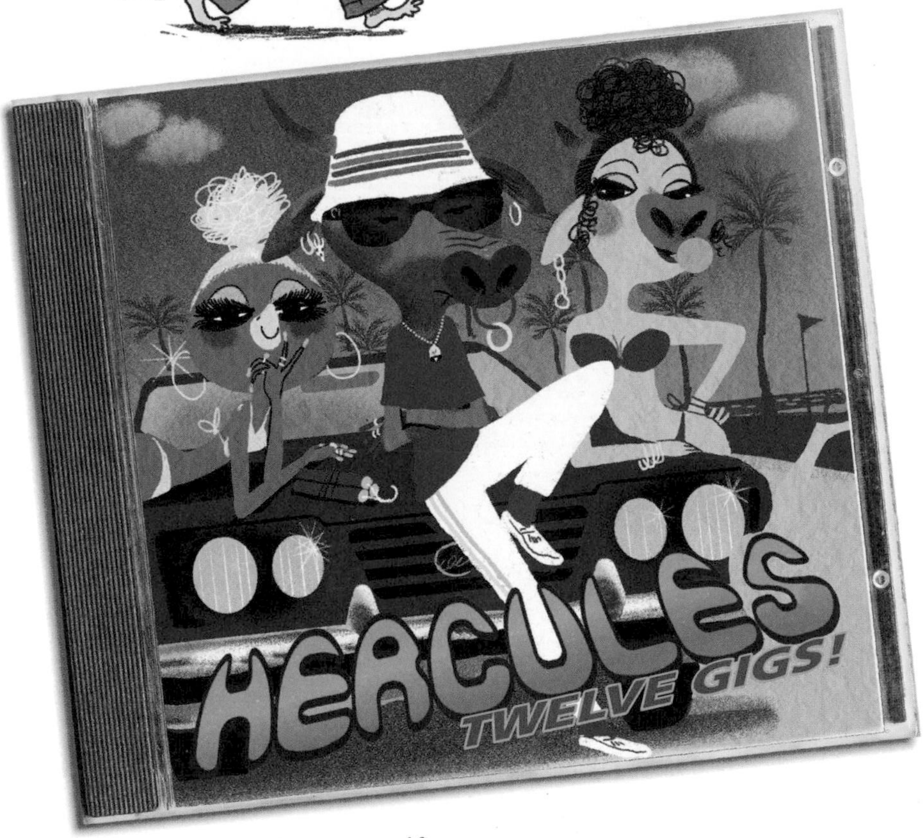
HERCULES
TWELVE GIGS!

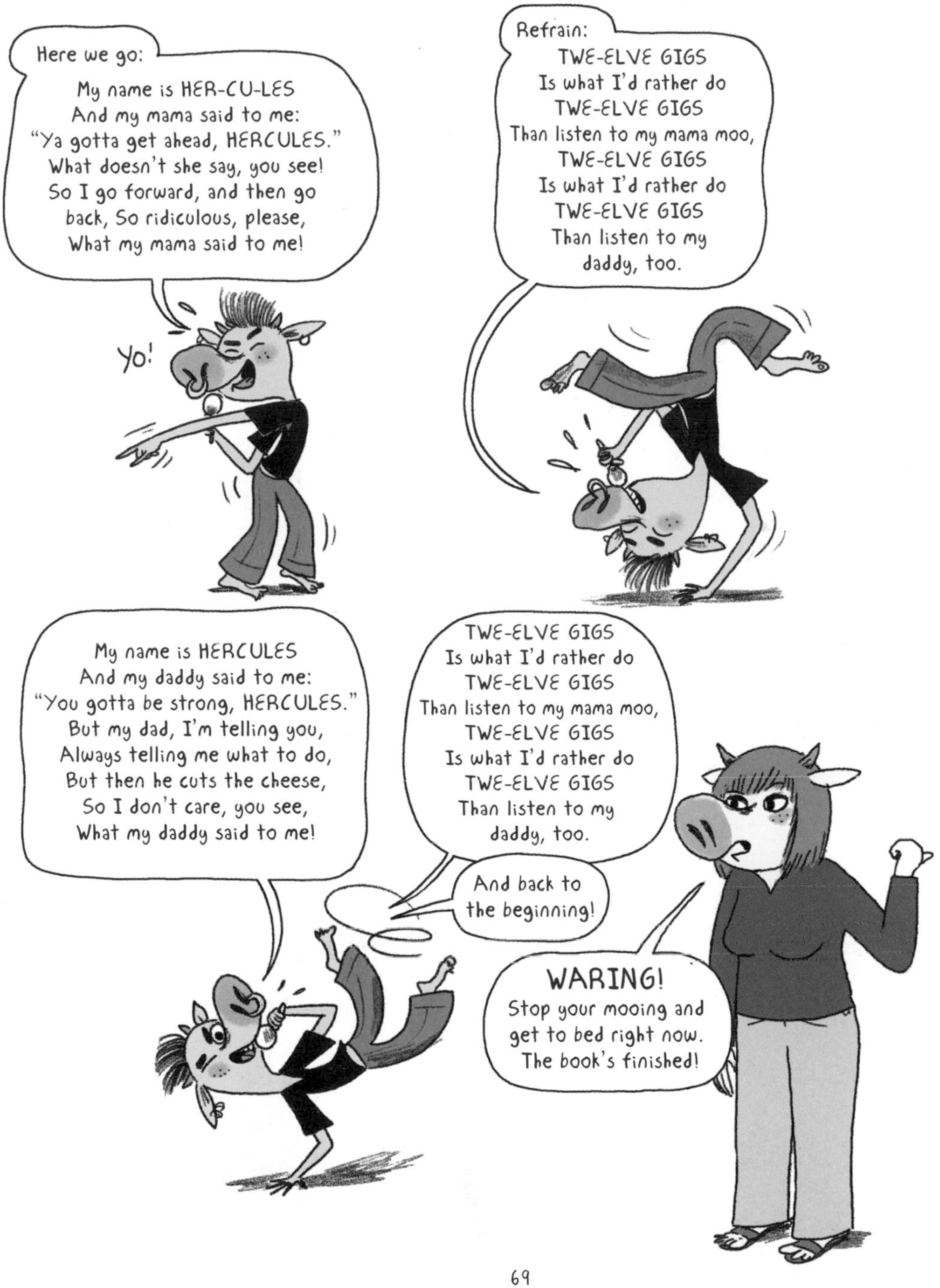
Here we go:
My name is HER-CU-LES
And my mama said to me:
"Ya gotta get ahead, HERCULES."
What doesn't she say, you see!
So I go forward, and then go
back, So ridiculous, please,
What my mama said to me!
Yo!
Refrain:
TWE-ELVE GIGS
Is what I'd rather do
TWE-ELVE GIGS
Than listen to my mama moo,
TWE-ELVE GIGS
Is what I'd rather do
TWE-ELVE GIGS
Than listen to my
daddy, too.
My name is HERCULES
And my daddy said to me:
"You gotta be strong, HERCULES."
But my dad, I'm telling you,
Always telling me what to do,
But then he cuts the cheese,
So I don't care, you see,
What my daddy said to me!
TWE-ELVE GIGS
Is what I'd rather do
TWE-ELVE GIGS
Than listen to my mama moo,
TWE-ELVE GIGS
Is what I'd rather do
TWE-ELVE GIGS
Than listen to my
daddy, too.
And back to
the beginning!
WARING!
Stop your mooing and
get to bed right now.
The book's finished!

Other Great Titles From PAPERCUTZ™

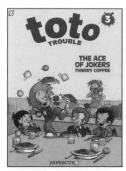

TOTO TROUBLE © Éditions Delcourt; CLASSICS ILLUSTRATED TM & © FIRST CLASSICS
INC.; DANCE CLASS and DINOSAURS © BAMBOO EDTION. ALL RIGHTS RESERVED.; DISNEY
FAIRIES © DISNEY ENTERPRISES; THEA STILTON © ATLANTYCA SPA. ALL RIGHTS RESERVED.
ERNEST & REBECCA © ÉDITIONS DU LOMBARD (DARGAUD-LOMBARD S.A.) THE GARFIELD
SHOW © Dargaud Media.

 © Peyo - 2015 - Licensed through Lafig Belgium

And Don't Forget . . .
All-new, full-color Graphic Novel
Thea Stilton
THE TREASURE OF THE VIKING SHIP
PAPERCUTZ
SMURFS STORY BY Peyo
THE FINANCE SMURF
PAPERCUTZ
...available at your favorite booksellers.

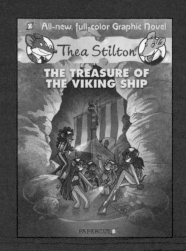

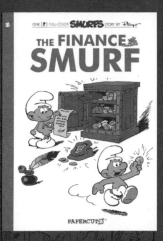

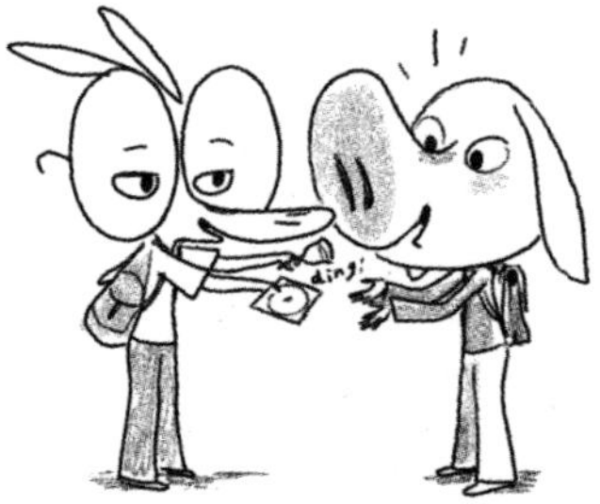
ding!